Music for Hard Times

MUSIC FOR HARD TIMES

new & selected stories

CLINT McCOWN

Press 53
Winston-Salem

Press 53, LLC
PO Box 30314
Winston-Salem, NC 27130

First Edition

Cover art, "Fire Lake," Copyright © 2020 by Clint McCown

Cover design by Kevin Morgan Watson

Library of Congress Control Number
2021932347

Printed on acid-free paper
ISBN 978-1-950413-35-5

for
Mallie *&* Caitlin
Dawn *&* Amber
the gifted sources of my great good fortune

ACKNOWLEDGMENTS

Earlier versions of these stories, sometimes under other titles, first appeared in the following places:

American Fiction, 1991, "Home Course Advantage"
American Fiction, 1993, "Mule Collector"
Colorado Review, "History Lessons," "But Then Face to Face,"
   "Cheap Imitations"
Gettysburg Review, "Whirlwind," "Surface Tension"
Hunger Mountain, "Once Upon a Time, a Scavenger"
Northwest Review, "Survivalists"
Sewanee Review, "Music for Hard Times"

"Home Course Advantage" was awarded the 1991 American Fiction Prize, judged by Louise Erdrich.

"Mule Collector" was awarded the 1993 American Fiction Prize, judged by Wallace Stegner.

"The Last Warm Day in Alabama" appeared in a different form in *The Weatherman*, published by Graywolf Press. All other stories also appeared in different forms in either *The Member-Guest* (Doubleday), *War Memorials* (Graywolf Press, Houghton Mifflin), or *Haints* (New Rivers Press).

I'm grateful to the following for their creative input and un-wavering spiritual support over the years: David Jauss, Bret Lott, David Wojahn, Keith Ratzlaff, Jeff Gundy, Kevin Stein, Jim Peterson, Mark Cox, Ralph Angel, Mary Ruefle, and Curt Musselman & Cecelia Brown. My thanks to Virginia Common-wealth University, which provided me with time to work on this collection; and to Kevin Morgan Watson, who does more than his share in keeping literature alive in the world; and to dear old Wake Forest—thine is a noble name.

CONTENTS

CHEAP IMITATIONS

At first the lizard was just one more source of tension between us. Laney bought it secondhand from some woman down in Huntsville who said it kept her cockroach problem under control. She told Laney it was a fine lizard, whatever that means, and she flat hated to sell it but she was just about to get married and didn't think she'd need a lizard anymore. I guess we all start out with high expectations.

I have to admit, this wasn't just a spur-of-the-moment purchase on Laney's part. We'd seen a TV news show about how people in New York kept geckos in their apartments to eat the insects, and right then Laney said she wanted one. Then when the carpenter ants showed up in the pantry, she brought it up again. I still didn't take her seriously.

I mean, some problems you can live with for a pretty long time—or at least I can. Maybe that's one of my many flaws. And to be fair, it got to where we couldn't turn on a light in a dark room without setting off a cockroach stampede. So Laney wasn't wrong, we'd reached a kind of tipping point where something had to be done. But big lizards weren't exactly the pet of choice in our part of the country. It never occurred to me that she might actually go out and find one of the damned things.

And, strictly speaking, she didn't. This particular lizard was no gecko. The previous owner said it was something *like* a gecko, but not a gecko exactly. I tried to look it up in a couple of reptile books, but I never could find a picture of it. So I don't know what the hell it was. Just some big lizard. Laney paid two hundred dollars for it.

That bothered me—two hundred bucks for some off-brand lizard. It was ugly, too. Fat and brown and bumpy, like a miniature fire log with legs. And slow. Real slow. The poor bastard couldn't catch a cockroach if its life depended on it.

Its name was Randall.

Well, right from the start Laney acted like Randall was the best thing that had come into her life in the last ten years. He was all she talked about. Randall was so cute. Randall was so friendly. Randall was so clever. Turn the air conditioner down— Randall might catch a chill. Keep those cupboard and closet doors open—Randall needs to explore his space. Don't use insect spray—Randall might swallow a contaminated bug. Watch where you step, watch where you sit, watch when you flush. She bought him little lizard treats at the pet store—reconstituted fly pellets, or some such abomination. She bought him little sticks and bells to play with, and little ladders to climb on, and little padded boxes to sleep in. She spent vast stretches of time scratching his head, and stroking his tail, and talking baby talk to him. She even made him a goddamned sweater.

To Randall's credit, he never went for any of it. Laney was just one more piece of odd weather as far as he was concerned. That was one of the things I liked about him.

And I did like him. He wasn't cute, or friendly, or clever, or affectionate, or any of the other things Laney imagined him to be. But he was stoic. I had to give him that.

So I guess Randall turned out to be a pretty versatile pet. Laney liked him because he had the sort of personality she could relate to. I liked him because he had no personality at all.

Anyway, on the day me and Dell found Jerry Moffit's body slumped over in his living room chair, we had to put in a twelve-hour shift. Not because of Jerry—we didn't officially involve ourselves in that headache. We just loaded the appliances on the truck and headed back to the warehouse, where Dell made an anonymous phone call to the proper authorities. Dell had been in the repo business long enough to know how to handle a situation like that. So Jerry didn't slow us down, is what I'm saying. No, the shift was a long one because of the time of year. Early summer is the prime season for repo work. For one thing, there's more afternoon light to work by, and believe me, only a fool tries to do our kind of labor after dark. The other reason is contractual: summer is when all the Christmas credit runs out.

That means we have to take back all those expensive holiday presents guilty husbands gave their wives. Jerry was a case in point. He must have figured a new washer and dryer would lure Charlene back home. But buying something you can't pay for only makes the hole you're in deeper. You'd be amazed at how many people don't understand that. If some divorce lawyer followed us door-to-door after Memorial Day, he could pick up enough business to retire on.

I don't know why people spend their money like they do. Why does a man who makes ten bucks an hour heaving feed sacks off a loading dock try to give his wife a full-carat diamond ring? What the hell is he thinking? I guess it's a way to buy time, if the marriage is shaky. But that's a fool's bet. The benefits only last until the payments come due. If anybody asked my opinion, I'd say cubic zirconia makes more sense. Gaudy as a diamond but only fifty bucks. No repo men at the door.

Our family room was a different matter altogether. No shortcuts there—no cheap materials, no shoddy workmanship. But there was a reason to go first-class on a job like that. This wasn't just a cosmetic fix-up; it was a legitimate investment, one that would have raised our property values, one that would have paid us back if we ever sold.

Would have.

When I got home Monday evening, it was already half twilight and I felt drained—and not just from hauling refrigerators and such. It was hard to stop thinking about Jerry Moffit. One thing that weighed on me was that I couldn't talk about any of it to Laney, unless I was ready to explain what I was doing in Jerry's house to begin with, and I sure as hell wasn't ready to throw that log on the fire. If I told Laney I was doing repo work for Hometown Finance, I'd also have to tell her I'd lost my job at the insurance agency—that my father had fired me for forging his name on a backdated rider to our homeowner's policy. And then she'd want an explanation for that, and I'd have to tell her I forgot to update our policy when we built the new family room, which meant we weren't covered for the oak tree that came through the roof last month when we had the big thunderstorm. A series of bad breaks, that's all it was, but I doubted Laney would see it that way, so I just kept my mouth shut. I know all the magazines say to be open and honest with your spouse, but that's not the universe I live in.

I stood there in the front yard for a while looking at the strange glimmering outline of my house—the right side all trim and proper, the left side a splintered pile of bones. Perfect opposites. Like before and after.

Like his and hers.

Laney's car was gone, so at least I didn't have to worry about excuses. I walked up to the demolished addition and climbed through where the picture window used to be. There really wasn't much left of the project but a partial outline and a few jagged piles of debris. And shadows because the sun was almost down. It was like stepping into a combat zone, like I was suddenly in one of those TV news pieces about bombed-out villages in eastern Europe somewhere, or even one of my father's cities from the war.

This was the room where Jerry Moffit should have died.

I maneuvered around the wreckage to the battered kitchen doorway. The frame was so off-level now, the door dragged on the linoleum, but I was able to wedge it open enough to squeeze inside. The place was nearly dark—we've got a row of old hackberry trees along the west side of the yard, so dusk falls heavy throughout the house—and for just a second I felt like I was still on the job, creeping into some deadbeat's boarded-up home. But this particular half-darkness was all mine, and I felt comfortable enough to move around in it without turning on any lights.

The eyes do adjust, after all. People tend to forget that. My mother used to start turning on lights in the middle of the afternoon, like she was afraid the darkness might sneak up on her. But I like the way darkness drifts into a room like smoke. I like the way it gathers unevenly around the furniture and along the walls, going dark, darker, darkest. I bet the pioneers used to watch the night come down like that. We don't do that anymore—not many of us anyway. Edison weakened our talent for living in the dark. We've lost patience, or at least that's the way it's gone for Laney and me. The dark used to be an interesting place. Now we just sleep there.

Here's something I wonder: Is there such a thing as the speed of darkness? I had a physics class in high school, and all Mr. Tucker ever seemed to talk about was Einstein and relativity and the speed of light. I was never too bright a bulb in the sciences, but I could pretty much follow what he was telling us. I mean, I couldn't do the math or anything, but I could still get the gist of the ideas. And one of the things he kept on about was how Einstein thought the speed of light was the only constant in the universe. That sounded okay to me at first, but then I started thinking—how could you say the speed of light was constant unless you had some other constant to measure it by? I mean, if you're zipping along in an airplane looking out at the clear blue sky, you can't tell how fast you're going. For all you know, you might be stopped dead still in a headwind. Hell, you might be going backwards. Landscape's the key—you can't figure speed without it. Let a few trees and houses go by, then you can start to calculate things. So wouldn't the same rules have to apply to light? I mean, if Einstein, or whoever, says light goes by at 186,000 miles per second, doesn't that mean there has to be something else in the neighborhood stuck on zero? And wouldn't that zero always have to be darkness? And wouldn't that mean darkness was a universal constant, same as light?

I tried to have a conversation with Laney about that one night. I told her I thought the speed of darkness had to be zero, or else the speed of light would just be a made-up number. She said she thought it wouldn't be too long before somebody invented a time machine, like in the movies. She said she looked forward to that. She wanted to try out the future.

I know what both my grandmothers would have said if I told them darkness was a universal constant. They'd have said I ought to go to church more. In our county, Jesus was the only universal constant that mattered.

Jesus. Jesus Christ. Jesus Christ our Lord and Savior. Jesus H. Christ.

When I was four years old I thought Jesus was one of the stock boys at the A&P. It was an easy mistake to make. For one thing, he wore a plastic name tag that said *Jesus,* and that was the one word Grandmother Vann had already taught me to read. He had a beard like Jesus. He even had a job like Jesus—always helping people out with the right directions so they could find the things they needed. Plus, there was this big curved mirror in the back of the store so he could see down every aisle at once, and from what I understood, that was just like Jesus, too. I remember running up to Grandmother Vann in the fruit and vegetable section and telling her I'd found Jesus. At first she got this serious-happy look and hugged me tight like I'd just been snatched from the jaws of Hell. "Praise the Lord!" she said, and things might have been

fine if she could have let it go at that. But my grandmother was
a woman who always needed to know the details, so she pressed
me for the full account. I told her what I knew—that Jesus was
unpacking canned peaches back by the meat counter—and then
watched her face turn dark and unfamiliar. She jerked me across
her knee so fast it made my bones rattle, and then she beat the
backs of my bare legs with a handful of celery stalks.

That's when I first started to catch on that Jesus was not
exactly a one-size-fits-all proposition.

I pulled open the pan drawer in the bottom of the stove and
fished around in the darkness for a pot to boil water in. Laney
had probably found dinner somewhere else, but I figured I'd still
cook up some macaroni and cheese, just to make the gesture.
Our good pot, the one we normally made macaroni and cheese
in, was still down at the Elks Lodge, where we'd left it after the
Memorial Day picnic, so I had to settle for the crummy one
I'd bought Laney for our third anniversary. The whole set was
crummy, not just the pot. All the pieces had that nonstick coating
that's supposed to be so easy to clean, but this was the cheap
version and the coating flecked off just about every time you
touched it. Macaroni always came out looking like it had been
rolled in pepper. I guess we should have thrown the set out, but
instead we kept it for things like baked beans, or turnip greens,
or black-eyed peas—dark foods, where the flecks wouldn't show.
God knows how much nonstick coating we've both got in our
systems by now.

I ran some water into the pot, letting the sound and the feel
of it tell me how much was enough, and then I carefully set it
on the front burner of the stove top. The house was totally dark
now, but my eyes had adjusted, so when I turned on the heat,
the red glow of the element gave me enough light to find the
box of macaroni in the cupboard. But then while I waited for
the water to boil, a burning smell began to fill the kitchen.

Laney and I aren't tidy cooks. We both tend to spill a lot of
food around the stove top, and hardly a day goes by that one
of us doesn't let something bubble over onto a hot burner. Our
drip pans are always crusty with mistakes. That's a fire hazard,
I realize, and we probably ought to pay higher insurance rates
because of it. But the only insurance man I know who'd actually nail us for it is my father, so what the hell. I sure don't plan
on having him to dinner any time soon.

Anyway, there must have been a little too much buildup around this particular burner, and now there was an acrid stink coming from whatever leftovers were being cooked away. Nothing flamed up, but I could feel the smoke clouding into my eyes. Since the exhaust fan was broken, I leaned across the sink and lifted the window to air things out a little. Then I turned off the burner and circled through to the third bedroom to raise the window in there to get some cross-ventilation going.

That room was where we stored the furniture Laney inherited from her maternal grandmother. Well, *inherited* might not be the right word. What I mean to say is that when Miss Bessie finally moved into the nursing home, Laney was one of the first family members to show up at her house with a pickup truck. Sometimes Laney wrote letters in here at Miss Bessie's old rolltop desk, but other than that we didn't really use the space.

I guessed this would be the baby's room.

A breeze got drawn in right away, and I stood there holding the window up and letting that cool night air bathe some of the smoke from my eyes. I had to hold the window in place because it would have dropped shut otherwise. All the windows in the house had gone crazy on us after the oak tree hit—I guess the frames got jarred out of plumb. Now the ones that used to slide easily got stuck all the time, and the ones that used to wedge in place came down like guillotines. We had to keep paint sticks on the sills so we could prop the loose ones open.

But this time there was no paint stick there. I held the lower sash up with one hand, and with the other I groped along the narrow top of Miss Bessie's desk, figuring that was the next most likely place Laney would have left it. I was right, but the dark made me too clumsy, and I bumped the stick off the back edge. It clattered down behind the rolltop.

That desk was massive, and I had no interest in moving it just to retrieve a fifteen-cent paint stick. Instead, I took the easier option—while I held the left side of the sash in place, I shoved up hard on the right side, forcing the window out of alignment with the frame. It worked: the lower sash wedged in place.

As I stepped back from the window, a car passed by the front of the house and the headlights swept through the room. That's when I noticed the rolltop desk was closed.

I'd never seen it closed before. The thing was nearly a hundred and fifty years old—Miss Bessie's grandfather had had it shipped over from England in the early 1800s, and then he carried it from New York to Tennessee in the back of a wagon. That's a lot of rough mileage for such a heavy piece of furniture. None of the joints were square anymore, and over the years a lot of the wood had warped. It was in sad shape overall, but the slatted rolltop was in particular need of repair. It just wouldn't ride the tracks anymore, not unless you forced it every inch of the way. Years ago I'd suggested to Miss Bessie that she might want to get it fixed, but she was afraid to let anybody tamper with it. Some fellow had told her that if you did anything to improve the condition of an antique, it wasn't a true antique anymore. And that meant it wasn't worth as much money.

The whole notion sounded wrong to me. How could a thing be worth more if you left it broken?

Anyway, the desk never got worked on and the top stayed open all the time, first in Miss Bessie's front parlor, and then here in the room where Laney would probably put the mystery child. So unless that fallen tree trunk had miraculously fixed the rolltop the way it had fixed some of our window frames—which was doubtful—Laney had gone to an awful lot of trouble to shut something up inside.

The fact that she'd even bother with it was surprising. Laney knew I wasn't the kind of person to snoop around in someone else's affairs—even hers. Invasion of privacy is a moral violation in my book—although a lot of folks I know would put it in the gray area because it isn't listed in the Ten Commandments. But for me it fits under the umbrella of the Golden Rule. If you look at the New Testament as a sort of insurance policy with God, the "Do unto others" passage is the most comprehensive subclause in the entire contract. And Miss Bessie's closed rolltop was one more case where the rule applied. I didn't want to know Laney's secrets any more than I wanted her to know mine.

However.

I pressed my palms against the wooden slats and carefully pushed upward. The top slid a few inches, then snagged, then slid a few inches more. When I'd worked it about halfway up, I stopped and peered inside. I couldn't see anything, of course, in that deeper darkness, but then I remembered that my wristwatch was the kind that lights up when you press a little button on the side. Laney had given me the watch last Christmas, before the whole Steve Pitts business got started. So I stuck my wrist into the cave of the rolltop and flooded the space with a pale green light.

There wasn't much there—a handful of ballpoint pens with insurance logos on the side, a box of rubber bands, a stapler, an unopened box of thank you cards that I recognized as left over from Laney's last birthday, a dog-eared stack of letterhead stationery from my father's office, and a straight-edged ruler with the agency's slogan printed in bold: *We Measure the Future.* Except for the thank you cards, it was all stuff I'd stolen from work the day I got fired.

The top sheet of letterhead had writing on it, so I aimed my watch face down at the page and leaned in close to see what I could make out. *Darling Steve,* it started, and I turned out the light.

Not that I hadn't expected to find such a thing, but still the sight of it hollowed me out like a paper bag. A love letter from my wife to her boyfriend, discovered by me through an act of personal depravity, stashed among office supplies I'd pilfered from my father: that was a pretty complete summary of my life to the present moment, and I felt sick to know it. If I'd dropped dead on the spot, the newspaper could have skipped the obituary and just run a snapshot of me with my head stuck in this goddamned desk. The Nolan Vann Memorial Portrait.

But after a few slow breaths, once the sound of my own heart had stopped echoing in my ears and my arm had stopped shaking, a spiteful recklessness set in, and I decided to descend a few rungs further. I shone the watch back onto the page and continued reading.

I don't know what to do, the letter began.

Below that, starting a new paragraph, was a second *I don't know what to do,* and below that, in nearly identical script, a third. Scanning down the page, I saw that Laney had filled the whole sheet with this one phrase, copying it out over and over, like a classroom punishment etched on a chalkboard: *I don't know what to do, I don't know what to do, I don't know what to do.*

Even taking into account that Steve Pitts was her audience, it was a pretty simple letter. I liked it, though. It had some good things to say, if you read between the lines.

But the feeling of recovery that had begun to rise up in me was interrupted now by a second sweep of headlights through the room—a partial sweep this time, freezing all the shadows into place as Laney's car pulled up in front of the house.

I'm not sure why I was slow to react. Maybe I was annoyed by the fact that she'd parked on the street again instead of in our driveway. I'd told her twenty times not to do that—a car by the curb was an open invitation to vandals; all the studies from the Underwriters Association had proven that. But Laney wouldn't listen. She hated to back out of the driveway because of some bushes in our neighbor's yard that blocked her view. She *said* they blocked her view, anyway. I never had any problem with them.

I watched her get out of the car and start up the sidewalk toward the house, then suddenly realized where I was and what I was doing. I gripped the bottom slats of the rolltop and tried to draw the cover back into place, but it wouldn't budge. There wasn't time to coax it down properly, so, in a slight panic, I rattled the top to loosen the jam, then yanked the whole thing toward me. Hard.

The bottom two slats came away in my hands, and a few more clattered to the floor in a god-awful racket.

I looked immediately to the yard and saw Laney stop dead-still halfway up the sidewalk. She stared at the window between us, her head cocked slightly to the side, listening. A dog in the next block began to bark, while the crickets and tree frogs went quiet. I knew she couldn't see me—the moon and the streetlights made the yard a relatively brighter place—so I kept still myself to see what she would do.

At first she didn't do anything but stand there, a vague outline in the early night. Vague, but still striking, still unmistakably Laney, and I felt a slight grief as I tried to separate her face from the darkness.

Her face.

In junior high we used to have pep rallies—with the girls in the bleachers on one side of the gym and the boys on the other—and I could pick her out right away, every time, without even trying. My eyes just automatically moved to wherever she was, even if she was sitting behind someone else, or had her head turned away.

That much hadn't changed. I could still recognize Laney anywhere, under any circumstances, in any degree of darkness. If there were such a thing as a group photo of the whole world, I swear I could spot Laney's face in the crowd a full year before I could ever find my own.

If I saw two people's shadows mingled on a motel window shade, I'd know which half was hers.

And maybe there really had been some kind of hokey, half-baked true love behind it all, at least on my part: some natural flutter in the chest that gave me this unasked-for ability to see through all the clutter and the dark to wherever Laney might be.

Or maybe I was wrong. Maybe this talent I had was nothing but an instinct for survival, some animal sense that instantly locked my attention on the thing that held the greatest threat.

Either way, it had always been scary to take my eyes off her.

"Hello?" she called out. "Nolan?" She left the sidewalk and edged slowly toward the window. "Nolan, are you home?"

I don't know why I couldn't answer. Something about the word *home* seemed to trip me up.

"I know somebody's in there," she said as she moved her face up close to the screen. "And I don't mind calling the sheriff."

I barely breathed. Soon her eyes would adjust and she'd see me standing in the darkened baby's bedroom. She'd ask what the hell was going on, and I wouldn't have an answer, not an easy one, anyway, because I wasn't sure myself what the hell was going on. Then she'd come storming inside and discover what I had done to her grandmother's desk. I didn't know what to do.

I didn't know what to do.

Then a remarkable thing happened. Just at the moment when I thought there was no way around it, when I thought there was no choice left but to speak up and let Laney know that I was there, that she had caught me, that I had broken Miss Bessie's antique rolltop, that I had read the letter, that I knew about Steve Pitts, that I'd known about Steve Pitts, in fact, ever since I'd spotted Laney's car at the Stone Bridge motel last Valentine's Day when she was supposed to be visiting her sister and—what the hell, why stop there—that I'd never insured our new family room and had no money to pay for the damage, that I was barely on speaking terms with my father, that I'd lost my job at the agency and was now a part-time repo man, that I'd found a dead body at work, that I knew the baby probably wasn't mine, but—sure, why not say it—that Laney still looked good, damned good, even after all these years, even in the goddamned dark—just as I was on the verge of saying all that and more, maybe a whole lot more, about junior high and the speed of light and how I didn't believe a thing could be worth more if you left it broken, just at that very moment, Randall the secondhand lizard waddled out onto the windowsill between us.

Apparently, he'd been lounging along the back of the over-stuffed chair next to the window, and the sound of Laney's voice had drawn him forward. So as she cupped her hands around her eyes and peered into the room, it wasn't me she focused on but Randall, perched calmly behind the screen, inches from her face, waiting for Laney to give him a cricket.

Laney's tone changed at once. "Randall," she cooed, "what have you been up to in Mommy's room?"

So that's what this place was.

"You just wait right there," she said. "I'll bring you some goodies."

As Laney moved from the window toward the front porch, I tried to map out a plan. My first idea—which was all I had time for—was to get to one of the other bedrooms and flop down on the bed like I was asleep. That would explain why the lights were out and why I didn't answer Laney's calls. I'd just have to claim ignorance about the rolltop.

As Laney opened the front door and turned on the living room lights, I set the broken slats gently into the cavity of the desk and hurried toward the hallway. But just as I turned the corner to make my escape, Laney swung the front door solidly shut behind her and a shiver of vibration passed through the house.

A second slam came from the room behind me, from the baby's room, the room where Bessie's antique desk had just grown a few decades older.

I knew what it was, of course, but I still had to turn back and look. And sure enough, there was Randall, his chunky body sticking up from the sill at an odd angle, his head wedged beneath the heavy fallen sash. I crossed quickly to the window and lifted the weight from his neck, but it was too late. After a couple of spasms jolted through his legs, he went limp. I held him up and looked into his eyes for some flicker of life, but there was nothing there. His mouth was opened wide, and for the first time since I'd known him he seemed to have an actual expression on his face. He looked surprised.

I probably did, too, when Laney walked into the room and turned on the light.

HOME COURSE ADVANTAGE

Even while he was gluing the new set of grips on Mrs. Davies's
old Patty Berg irons, Rod could't stop thinking about the
carcass of the dog. The dewfall would have settled over it by
now, which he hoped might dampen the smell. In the three days
since he'd cut too sharply into the parking lot and caught the
mangy stray unawares, the temperature had seldom slipped
below ninety. This morning a couple of the club members had
complained. The odor, they said, had been sucked in through
their car air conditioners. They wanted it taken care of. The
member-guest tournament was just a few days away, and a lot
of out-of-towners would be coming in for practice rounds. It
didn't speak well of the club to leave a dead dog at the entrance
to the parking lot.

So Rod had called the highway department to see if they'd
come out and get the thing. They said they would, but it might
take a couple of weeks—most of their trucks were tied up in
the Route 15 bypass project, and roadkill had become a low
priority. He told them he'd take care of it himself, and as he
hung up the phone he made a mental note to pass the chore on
to the Wickerham kid, who was running the grounds crew this
summer.

But then the special shipment of Izods arrived, the one he'd
ordered to beef up his sweater stock before the member-guest
weekend, and he had to check the merchandise for damage.
When he'd finally logged in all the stock numbers, he set to
work assembling the eight-foot cardboard alligator they'd sent

as a new promotional display. He was still trying to insert tab M into slot Q when Beverly Cooper came in from the snack shop to tell him the freezer unit was making clacking noises and defrosting itself again. It took him half the afternoon to track down Ed Betzger, who held the service contract on all the club's appliances, and by the time Ed had the unit working again, the ice cream bars were showing clear signs of strain. So Rod had to call Teddy Mumford, the club's insurance agent, to find out how far the meltdown had to go before the bars could be claimed as a loss. Here there was a point of contention: Teddy said that partial melting didn't constitute spoilage, and as long as the ice cream was uncontaminated it could still be sold. Rod explained that the bars didn't even look like bars anymore, but Teddy said the snack shop could feature them on the menu as a novelty item. Refrozen ice cream sounded exotic, Teddy told him, like refried beans. Rod said maybe it was time the club got a new insurance agent.

Of course, that would never happen. Rod ran the daily operations of the club, but the board of directors made all the financial decisions; and Teddy Mumford was a member of the board.

The injustice galled Rod, and as soon as he got off the phone with Mumford he stormed into the men's locker room to air a few complaints. But it was late in the day, and there was no one there but Glen L. Hanshaw, himself one of the oldest board members, sitting naked on the bench in front of his locker. It was a disconcerting sight, and Rod lost his momentum.

"Look at this crap!" Glen L. said, and he held up a pair of boxer shorts. "I haven't had these a goddamn month and the elastic's all shot to hell." He threw them into the bottom of his locker and slammed the door closed with his foot. "I swear to Christ!"

Rod didn't know what to say, so he looked at his watch and hurried on down the row of lockers.

"Hey, wait a minute!" Glen L. pushed himself up from the bench and followed Rod to the side door. In the diffuse light of the windows, his skin took on a bluish pallor, like a body washed up from the sea. "I had a complaint about you today," he said.

"What's the problem?"

"Shirley Davies says you were supposed to get her clubs back to her two weeks ago."

"The new grips haven't come in yet," he lied.

"Well, she was all over my ass about it." He ran a bony hand over his scalp. "I hear she's having trouble at home. Probably just needs to take it out on somebody. Anyway, I told her you'd take care of it."

Rod shrugged. "I'll see what I can do."

"Good man." Glen L. slapped him on the shoulder and padded off toward the showers. He moved unnaturally, Rod thought, as if he were picking his way across hot gravel. Strange what nakedness could do to some people. In his loud shirts and double-knit pants, Glen L. was the tyrant of his Cadillac dealership; here at the club, all the kids who worked in the pro shop were afraid of him. But now he seemed just one more small animal caught outside its territory. Rod didn't know why, but the thought depressed him.

He climbed the stairs to his workroom and set about regripping Mrs. Davies's old irons. He got out the new grips and settled in on his bench by the window to start stripping the shafts. Only then did he remember that he'd never spoken to Jimmy Wickerham about getting rid of the dog. Now it was too late—the last few twilight stragglers were just coming in off the course. The grounds crew would have left hours ago. If Rod wanted the carcass disposed of before tomorrow, he'd have to do it himself.

It took him longer than usual to do the re-gripping. Somehow he mispositioned two of the new grips and had to strip both shafts and start again. The seven iron gave him particular trouble. The glue had hardened in a lump where the left thumb gripped the shaft, and though he knew Mrs. Davies would never know the difference, he couldn't let the imperfection pass. The seven iron was his favorite club, the luckiest club. He'd once holed out a 170-yard approach shot with a seven iron on the final hole of the Doral Open. The eagle jumped him up to eighth place, his best professional finish.

By the time he was satisfied with the positioning of all ten grips, it was after ten o'clock. He turned out the workshop light and stood for a minute by the window facing the highway. It was a moonless night, but the mercury vapor lamp above the machine shed cast a yellow haze across the deserted parking lot. The dog lay just inside the edges of the light, and Rod could see clearly the dark lump waiting for him on the carpet of manicured grass.

But what exactly was he supposed to do with it?

He couldn't just sling it into the clubhouse dumpster. The container wouldn't be emptied until Tuesday, and five days of dumpster heat was the last thing this dog needed.

He couldn't dump it anywhere on the course because the grounds were kept so immaculately trimmed it was impossible to hide anything larger than a golf ball. The only exception was the bramble thicket that ran along the out-of-bounds to the left of the third hole, but that entire stretch was usually upwind from most of the course, and there was too much stink left in the animal to risk it.

He sure as hell wasn't about to load the remains into the back of his new Audi and go cruising around the countryside looking for a safe drop zone. He'd bought that car because he thought it might foster an image of stability and class, and he was certain that a lingering bad-meat smell would undercut his efforts.

Of course he could always take the Teddy Mumford approach of cheapskate practicality: run the carcass through the wood chipper and spray the remains along the fairways for fertilizer. Even as he laughed at the thought, he felt a twinge of guilt toward Teddy. Mumford wasn't such a bad guy, really; he was just trying to keep the club's premiums low. It had been a heavy year for claims against their current policy—there'd been some major plumbing and electrical problems, a fire in the women's locker room, vandalism on two of the greens, and a lot of theft. In the last two weeks alone they'd lost over eighteen thousand dollars' worth of equipment: three electric Cushman golf carts and a small tractor mower. The insurance rates were bound to go up. Teddy had even told the board that unless the club could find a way to hire a night watchman, the home office might not let him renew their policy at all.

Rod hoped they would hire a watchman. He also hoped they'd hire a club manager, an accountant, a full-time assistant for the pro shop, and a couple of bag boys to clean the members' clubs. Then maybe he'd have some time to work on his game. The way things stood now, he almost never got out on the course, and in the four years he'd been club pro, he'd lost a lot of ground. His putting was pretty much the same as ever—it came in streaks, and he rarely missed anything under five feet. But he'd lost some of his touch on the pitch-and-run shots, and even with his wedge he couldn't seem to make the ball bite the way it used to. His overall game was about four shots worse than when he'd started here. At that rate he'd be a duffer long before retirement age.

He knew it was his own fault. Nobody had forced him to take the job. In fact, he'd been happy to get it. The course had a good layout, and even though the club ran on a pretty tight budget, enough money went to maintenance to keep it one of the finest nine-hole operations in the state. He didn't have to be ashamed of working here. Besides, he'd gotten tired of running with the rabbits, of driving from tournament to tournament all season long, scrambling for some share in the winnings. In three years he'd made the cut nine times, and his career earnings wouldn't even cover his gas money. He quit the tour the week after the Doral Open, when his visibility was high enough to land him a steadier job. He didn't regret it. Even rookies had been finishing higher than Rod in the tournament standings, and the truth that sank into him after Doral was that eighth place was as high as he'd ever go.

It was just as well, he told himself. He loved the game, but he wasn't cut out for business, and success made a business out of any game. Suppose he'd won the U.S. Open, or the Masters, or the P.G.A.; corporations would've come beating down his door for endorsements. They'd have turned him into a "personality" and designed some ridiculous logo for his autographed line of leisurewear.

He did wonder what the logo might have been. Some animal, certainly—they were all animals. Alligators were already spoken for. So were penguins, seagulls, bears, jaguars, sharks, pandas, bulls, mustangs, dolphins, zebras, kangaroos, and flamingos.

No dogs, though, or at least none that he'd ever noticed— certainly no dead stray dogs: no bloody, bashed-in, half-breed German shepherds embroidered with infinite care into the tight weave of cotton-Orlon-Dacron acrylic. If he ever did hit the big time maybe that could be his logo. He might even insist on it.

He picked up Mrs. Davies's seven iron to double check the feel of it, and made his way downstairs and out the rear of the clubhouse. The night air was cool, and from the way the wind was gusting through the trees, he guessed a storm might be moving in. Long rolls of heat lightning shimmered across the southern sky.

The window of the machine shed was unlocked, as usual, and Rod had no trouble reaching in for the shovel he knew would be hanging on the inside wall. As he walked across the lot toward the dead dog, a feeling of lightness came over him. Once he got the creature in the ground, the whole affair would be over. He'd never have to think about it again.

The night, he soon discovered, was the best possible time for the work. He'd been right about the smell; without the constant prodding of the sun, the flesh had sunk back into a more passive state of decay, and the dew seemed to keep the odor from rising. Only occasionally did little stabs of corruption dart up on the breeze, and by keeping the wind at his back and breathing carefully, he was able to avoid most of the stench. The flies seemed to have settled down for the night—or maybe the wind was keeping them at bay—and, while there were probably slugs and other night-workers swarming the rotting underside, they were all invisible, hidden by dog or darkness, so Rod could work easily, with his eyes open, in a way that would have been difficult for him in the full light of day.

The one thing that did bother him was the collar.

From the moment the animal had sprawled with a single yelp under the front left tire, Rod had avoided looking at it closely. He'd glimpsed enough to know the dog was a mixed breed, and from its general scruffiness he'd assumed it to be a stray. Now a queasy fear came over him that he'd open the morning paper and find some pathetic plea for the return of a family pet: Lost, in the vicinity of Route 30 west of town, a brown-and-black dog, part shepherd, answers to the name of. . .

A silver tag gleamed in the pale light. On it, Rod knew, there would be some identification, but he couldn't bring himself to bend his face down close enough to read what the inscription might say. Instead, he carefully hooked the head of Mrs. Davies's seven iron underneath the collar and began to drag the dead dog toward the putting green. The body stayed perfectly curled, firm now as a piece of sculpture as it scraped along the gravel lot. The weight of the thing surprised him. Until now he'd thought of the carcass as just a husk, and it amazed him to realize that the dog was no less substantial for the fact of having died.

He circled below the putting green and drew the dog alongside the practice bunker. The raised lip between the bunker and the ground spread a less diluted night across the sand so that at first the trap seemed bottomless, a sinkhole yawning in the grassy slope. But soon his eyes adjusted, and the shadow gave way to the dingy sparkle of the sand itself. It was a perfect spot. The digging would be easy here, and when he was through there would be no broken turf to give the grave away.

He stepped down into the bunker and began shoveling the whiter top sand into a far corner to keep it separate from the brown foundation grit and the reddish dirt that lay below. It took him only six or seven minutes to work his way through the natural layer of topsoil, and though his progress slowed from the increasing density and rockiness of the ground, he continued to make headway.

It felt good to work the shovel in the earth, so good he started humming as he dug, improvising variations on a single jazzy theme for nearly half an hour, until suddenly, as he strained to pry loose a stubborn, buried stone, it came to him what the song was, and with that thought the sound of it died in his throat. It was a song that had haunted him for weeks now.

He didn't even know its name, but he took it to be an old blues number, maybe from the Billie Holiday era. The lyrics were hazy to him—some usual fare about love gone wrong— but what still burned in his mind was the one time he'd heard it, sitting in Herr's Tavern drinking his fourth double scotch, alone at a corner table in the otherwise crowded bar. A woman, heavily made up but still somehow breathtaking, swayed on a low platform by the far wall and sang, with her eyes closed, in the voice of a grieving angel. Even through the smoke and the room's dim amber glow, he could see that her hair was red, deep red, and it clung in damp curls to her cheek and forehead. Her pale skin seemed unearthly, perfect, fragile as glass. She poured herself like whiskey through the song, and Rod could have believed she was all the beauty left in the world; and that she was dying, now, in front of him. He envied her the grandeur of such public despair.

When her song was over, she opened her dry eyes and smiled warmly at the crowd, nodding to specific groups for their whistles and applause. Then her whole face brightened—she'd spotted someone particular at Rod's end of the room—and without hesitation she climbed awkwardly down from the makeshift stage, a long leg showing through the slit in her gown, and weaved her way between the tables toward him. He watched her intently as she moved, fascinated by the ease with which she'd left the song behind, like a snake shedding skin, or a butterfly, maybe, abandoning an outworn cocoon. It wasn't until she reached his chair that he realized he was the person she was crossing to meet, and before he could offer up any question she flung an arm around his neck and kissed him earnestly on the mouth. He was as stunned as if he'd been hit by a truck.

As she drew her face away from his, he opened his mouth to fumble toward some trite compliment about her singing, but before he could manage even a syllable a dark change came into her eyes, and she pulled herself up straight.

"My God," she said, her right hand fluttering to her cleavage. "You're not Randy!" A bubble of embarrassed laughter broke from her throat, then she turned abruptly toward the stage. "Hey, Marcie," she called. "Look at this guy!" Half the heads in the room turned in Rod's direction. "Doesn't he look just like Randy?"

A woman from a table near the bar seemed to struggle for a moment with the task of bringing Rod into focus, then sank back in a confused frown. "You mean that's not him?"

"Hell, no! Can you believe this? And Christ, I just gave him a big wet one." Several people laughed, and she turned again to Rod. "Sorry, Sugar. Thought you were somebody else." She patted him on the cheek and threaded her way casually to the bar.

Rod felt like she took his whole identity with her. It was as if, for a few accidental seconds, he'd seen himself through her eyes and found that he was utterly invisible, a man so bland he could enter a look-alike contest for himself and still come away the loser. A shudder ran through him, and a spinning rose in his head that nearly tipped him over. He left the tavern without finishing his drink.

By now he'd achieved a pit nearly three feet deep, which he judged sufficient. He tossed the shovel into the hole and sat heavily on the upper rim of the trap. He was more than winded; the work had turned nasty toward the end and now ropes of undeveloped muscle began to knot along his back. He probably wouldn't be able to swing a club for a week. Still, he felt a sense of accomplishment, and in his sudden stupor of exhaustion he felt less finicky toward the condition of the dog—though he resisted the impulse to pat its mangled head.

The wind was stronger now and felt good against the side of his face, but the change in weather worried him. The sky was a black sheet, but he sensed in the air itself that clouds were already swirling in thick and low, and if he didn't get the dog in the ground in a hurry, he might end up soaked when the bottom dropped out. He pushed himself up from the bank and grabbed Mrs. Davies's seven iron, which was still hooked under the collar. The dog slid easily down the slope to the edge of the grave.

"Roll over!" Rod said, and with a twist of the iron, the carcass disappeared into the hole. "Now, stay!" With some difficulty he retrieved the club, then tamped down the body with the shovel. The snug fit pleased him, though he felt somehow disconcerted that in the underground darkness he couldn't tell whether the dog had landed on its back or on its stomach. He even thought about getting a flashlight from the clubhouse to find out, but in the end, fatigue convinced him to let it go. The dog wouldn't care, so why should he?

He was just pouring in the first shovelful of dirt when a pair of headlights swept across him from the highway. He froze like a startled animal and watched a large flatbed truck wheel into the lot. It pulled up by the machine shed fifty yards away, and a burly man in overalls climbed down from the cab. Rod saw at once that the man was ill at ease. Body movement, after all, was Rod's specialty; he knew how to read imperfections in a stance, a turn, a swivel, a follow-through, and he watched this trespasser now with a coldly professional eye.

Whatever the guy was up to, it seemed to Rod that he needed lessons. There was a tightness in the man's shoulders, and he moved his head with a birdlike jerkiness as he scanned the dark outer reaches of the lot. Rod knew he was too far away to be seen, particularly by anyone standing so near the security light, so he kept still and let the blind stare pass through him. There was something appealing in this—in seeing without being seen, as if he were no more than a ghost—but the interest Rod had in that aspect of the situation was offset by the column of stench now rising from the pit at his feet. He set the shovel down gently in the sand and eased his way upwind to the cleaner, whiter corner of the trap. He was just crouching below the smooth cut of the lip when the man in the lot let out a loud, shrill whistle. Rod thought at first he'd been spotted, but then he realized that the man wasn't looking his way. He was turned toward the machine shed with his head cocked to the side as if he were listening for something.

Rod listened, too. Except for the wind rustling the trees, everything was quiet. Even the crickets and frogs from the drainage ditch behind the first tee had grown still under the expectation of rain.

Then the man whistled again, but instead of waiting for a response he reached in through the window of the truck and took out what appeared to be a small tackle box. The next few steps were all too predictable. After so many years of golf, Rod knew how to trace a trajectory, and had only to watch the swing itself to know where the ball would land. When the man walked to the rear window of the machine shed and climbed inside, Rod could only shake his head. God, how he hated amateurs.

He climbed out of the trap and walked across the parking lot to the truck, Mrs. Davies's seven iron in hand. For a moment he considered bashing in the windshield, but gestures like that were more dramatic than effective, and anyway it might hurt the club. Instead, he just took the keys from the ignition and walked calmly back to his bunker. It was a good first move, he told himself. Every match hinged on psyching out the opponent.

A minute later the front door of the shed swung open and one of the new Cushman gas-powered carts came nosing silently out. Apparently, the man had been unable to hotwire it, in spite of his tool kit, and he now trotted alongside the cart, pushing and steering at the same time. He maneuvered the Cushman into position behind the truck, then pulled out a pair of long planks from the flatbed and propped them in place as a ramp. After lining up the steering for a straight shot at the boards, he got behind the cart and heaved it forward. Rod thought this a foolish technique—the wheels could easily miss one of the rails or skid over the side halfway to the truck. But the man seemed unconcerned, and when the front left wheel did slip from its plank, he was able to hold the four-hundred-pound cart level as he walked it forward into the bed of the truck. Rod was glad he hadn't smashed this fellow's windshield.

As he watched the thief slide the planks back onto the truck, Rod wondered why he hadn't just slipped away to the clubhouse and called the police. What made him think he had to handle this himself? He'd always been a smart money player, always staying with the high-percentage shot, and he knew better than to try to clear a hazard when the odds told him to play up short. Still, it was too late to worry about it now. The time to think was before the shot, never mid-swing.

He took a golf ball from his pocket and dropped it into the spongy grass just off the apron of the practice green. Then he took a narrow stance almost directly behind the ball and opened the face of the seven iron. It was a trick he'd learned for putting extra loft on a club, and though he'd never used the shot in competition because it was too difficult to control, he'd always known it was there if he needed it. He took a full swing across the ball, playing it more or less like an extreme bunker shot, and with a sharp *click* it vanished upward into the night.

The man across the lot was just lashing the cart to the flatbed when the clean sound of contact froze him in place, still as a photograph. For a full four seconds he held his pose, listening into the darkness. Then with a loud metallic thunk, the ball came down on the hood of the truck. It broke the stillness like a starter's gun, and the man bounded into the cab of the truck, slamming the door behind him.

Rod walked forward into the light and crossed the parking lot in long, brisk strides, like a tournament leader approaching the eighteenth green. He paused by the rear of the truck and for a prolonged moment the two men stared at each other's reflections in the side-view mirror. At last the door swung open and the cart thief climbed slowly out.

He was bigger than he'd seemed from across the lot—maybe six-foot-five—and old enough that middle age had parceled his bulk evenly between muscle and flab. His face was round, almost childlike, with a dark, sparse beard that sprouted in random patches over his cheeks. As he faced Rod in the gravel, he tucked his hands in his overalls with an air of defiant calm. His mouth hung slightly open, and his dull eyes looked haggard, even in the dim light. Rod felt certain the man was not a golfer.

"Evening," he said. The man nodded and coughed, but didn't speak. "I notice you've got one of our carts here."

The man glanced to the cart, then took a studied look around him, as if he'd only that moment realized where he was.

"Yeah, well, we got a call to pick it up for some repairs. The transmission's gone bad."

"You work odd hours."

The man shrugged. "Some days are like that."

Rod reached up and touched the fiberglass body of the new

cart. "You know, I hate these bastards. They're an insult to the game."

"That so?" the man asked, nudging the gravel with the toe of his work boot.

"Yeah. They kill the grass. Most of the really good courses don't even allow them on the grounds." He shook his head at the cart, which gleamed in the glow of the vapor lamp. "But we're not exactly the Augusta National here, so I've got to put up with them. I even have to fix them when they break down. So I know you didn't get a call from anybody."

The man's slack-jawed pose fused into a more natural scowl.

"Then you must have my keys," he said, and started toward Rod, who shifted into a bunker stance and drew the seven iron to the top of his backswing.

"Buddy, I know how to use a golf club," he said. It was one of the few positive statements he could make about his life, and he was amazed at how little impact it had. The man hesitated for a moment—only for a moment—then with his eye fixed on the thin shaft of the iron, he gave a skeptical snort and lumbered into range.

The swing Rod used was smooth and relaxed—so much so that even the cart thief himself might have thought it a half-hearted effort. But the timing was there, and that's where the power lay in golf. There was a trick to it, like ringing the bell with a sledge hammer at the county fair. Rod rang the bell now. With a good body turn and a snap of his wrists, he transferred the entire momentum of his arc into the clubface. This was no stubby punch shot for getting out of tree trouble, but a full swing and follow-through, the kind that cuts down hard behind the ball and takes a deep, long divot. It did so now; the heavy blade caught the lower edge of the man's right kneecap and moved on through the shot for a clean, high finish.

With a startled gulp, the man tottered slowly sideways and crumpled to the rough pavement, too stunned at first to utter a sound. But that moment passed, and he launched into a shrill whine as he squirmed frantically on his crippled leg.

Rod stepped back to gauge the damage: the club was okay; the guy would be on crutches for a while. "I'm really sorry about this," he said.

The man glared up at him and spoke through clenched teeth. "I oughta kill you, you sonofabitch!" He looked as if he had more to say, but a fresh pain twisted through his leg and kept any words from forming. He turned his face away with a groan and began to rock back and forth in the gravel.

"I could call a doctor," Rod offered, but the man ignored him. He rolled onto his left side and whistled once more like he had when he'd first climbed down from the truck. The effort hurt him, and he groaned again. A queasiness rose up from the pit of Rod's stomach. "What are you whistling for?" he asked, though he thought he knew.

A strained smile broke across the man's face. "Somebody to tear your goddam arm off," he said, and fell into a giddy laugh.

"It's a dog, isn't it?" Rod asked.

"It's a bitch," the man answered, and he began to giggle uncontrollably. He leaned his weight back on his elbows and tried to straighten his leg in front of him, but the knee wouldn't unbend. "Christ," he said, still giggling. "What the hell have you done to me?"

"I think you've gone into shock," Rod told him.

The man lowered his head to the gravel and lay still as he could through the small spasms of laughter, taking slow, deep breaths until he finally brought the pain under control. At last he raised himself up and leaned heavily against the grimy rear wheel.

"What about the dog?" Rod asked.

The man sighed and stared down at his crooked leg. "She got away from me last week," he said.

"What the hell do you mean she got away from you?" The sharpness in Rod's tone surprised them both.

"I mean she jumped out of the truck to run down a rabbit," the man said, keeping a wary eye now on Rod's seven iron. "I couldn't wait around."

Rod hacked the club hard onto the pavement, sending up sparks and a small spray of stones. The man flinched and huddled closer to the wheel.

"You asshole," Rod shouted. "Don't you know better than to leave a dog to run loose by a highway?"

The man shrugged. "I came back," he said.

Rod hated simple answers. They weren't enough. Besides, they always seemed to back him into corners. For as long as he'd been part of the game, he could remember only two times when he'd given in to simple answers, and both times he felt cheated.

The first was when he was a boy, playing with his father's clubs. His father had been a left-hander, so for his first two years in the sport, Rod had been a left-hander, too. Then when he was twelve his father bought him a right-handed set. He was furious about having to start all over again, and he demanded a reason for his father's forcing him to give up so much ground. "You're not left-handed," his father told him.

The second time was when he decided to quit the tour.

He felt the same frustrations building up in him now, as if he were still somehow playing on the wrong side of the ball.

"You can keep the cart," he said.

The man narrowed his eyes. "What?"

"I said you can keep the cart. We've got insurance."

The man slowly pulled himself up on his good leg and steadied his weight against the side of the flatbed. "I don't know," he said, searching Rod's face for some sign of a trap. "That doesn't sound right. What's the catch?"

"I want you to give me your dog."

"What?"

"I want your dog."

The man looked around uneasily. "I told you, I already lost her."

"Then there shouldn't be any problem. From now on, we can just say she belongs to me."

"And that's it?"

"That's all."

The man chewed the inside of his cheek for a moment, and nodded. "Yeah, okay. Sure." Then he frowned. "What about my keys?"

Rod pointed to the darkness at the lower end of the lot. "There's a sand bunker just below that ridge," he said. "You might start looking down there."

The man eyed him suspiciously. "How am I supposed to do that? I can't even walk."

Rod extended the clubhead toward him. "You can have this."

The man reached carefully forward and took the iron from Rod's hand. "Okay," he said, then shifted his weight onto the shaft of the club and limped away from the truck. He circled wide around Rod and made his way cautiously toward the edge of the dark. Rod watched him until he reached the bunker, then took the keys from his pocket and tossed them through the open window of the cab.

He'd have to order Mrs. Davies a new seven iron. She'd be mad as hell when he told her he'd lost this one. She'd probably try to get him fired. But that was okay. Sometimes you just had to give up what you were used to, or you might never get anything right.

For now, though, the only thing he wanted to think about was hitting a bucket of range balls. He'd lost a little control lately, he knew that; and if he didn't work on it, his problems would only multiply. Golf was an unforgiving game, with no use for shortcuts or excuses. A good swing was built on fundamentals. The grip, the stance, the take-away, the follow-through—all had to be kept in balance. If one went wrong, the rest collapsed like a house of cards.

He would start with his wedge to see how his short game was holding up. Then he'd work his way right up through the driver.

But he'd have to hurry. The wind was rising stronger now and it swept in from the course with the clean smell of the coming storm. To the south he could see the glow of the town lights against the low-hanging clouds. The rain hadn't hit quite yet, but it would before long.

He knew it was bound to.

WHIRLWIND

As her mind bobbed gently to the surface and her eyelids fluttered open to the absolute darkness surrounding her, Mary Jean's first conscious thought was the worst: she was already dead and buried. Then she remembered the string of moments that had brought her here—Mr. Gatlin dangling her into the well as the twister bore down on them; her flailing about for a handhold and finding the rope ladder just as Mr. Gatlin released his grip; the clumsy descent, rung by rung, while the air howled overhead; and finally, the collapse onto the rocky floor of the well. She wasn't sure whether some trick of her pregnancy had diverted too much blood from her brain, or whether she had simply been overcome by fear, but whatever the case, a lightheadedness had swirled through her thoughts like water circling a drain, and she had fainted.

Apparently, she'd been unconscious for hours. The rainwater had nearly dried from the front of her dress, even in the chilly dank of the well bottom. Night had fallen, leaving her in the most total darkness she'd ever known. A stiffness had settled into her neck and back, probably from lying so long in a single, awkward position, and a chill ached through her bones. Her hip throbbed against a partly buried rock. Her left shoulder burned when she tried to lift her arm—she must have pulled a muscle when she'd first tumbled backward into the hole. The rear of her dress was soaked through, as if she'd sat in a puddle, though the ground around her felt only slightly damp beneath her fingers. She shifted her weight and began to grope with her right hand along the curve of the dirt wall, feeling for the ladder. When she found a rung, she pulled herself to her feet and stood there for a minute fighting a wave of dizziness and nausea. She had to hook her arm through the ladder to keep from sinking back to the floor of the well. The baby had never felt so heavy inside her.

Why had Mr. Gatlin left her alone?

She took a deep breath and let it out slowly. The last of her grogginess was lifting, and she felt certain she could scale the ladder in the dark, even in her present condition. But before her foot could find the first rung, a sudden cramping flared through her lower abdomen, and, with a quick gasp, she doubled over, scraping her cheekbone on the jagged wall. It occurred to her that her face was probably bleeding, but she didn't care, not now, not while this thing was happening. She wrapped her arms around her stomach and tried to take a breath, but a sob erupted in its place, followed by a long, low moan. Somewhere inside her a bare fist was squeezing a white-hot coal, and her whole being seemed to knot itself around the core. She must have hurt herself more seriously than she'd realized. She moaned again, louder this time, as the wave continued through her, battering whatever got in its way. She heard herself wail in the darkness.

And then, as abruptly as it had arrived, the wave subsided. The knot released itself, and all she felt was a cold, fresh layering of sweat.

"Mr. Gatlin!" she cried out. "I need some help!" She listened for a response, but none came. In fact, beyond the halting whisper of her own ragged breath, she heard no noises at all—no crickets, no wind, no pattering rain, no katydids buzzing in the leaves, no night owl sounding out its prey. For a second time, she wondered if she might be dead, wondered if her spirit might be lingering in some empty, silent limbo. Nothing in this world was familiar, nothing but the chill and the dark.

But something in the brittle stillness finally broke, and sound began to filter through from somewhere—faint and fragmented at first, but growing louder and clearer. Voices. She heard voices floating in the night air. She couldn't pick out any words, but someone was talking, she was sure of it. Two people, coming closer.

"I'm here," she called. "I'm in the well."

The voices stopped.

"I'm here!" she cried again.

She grabbed the rough rope and began to pull herself up the ladder. The climb was difficult without the use of her left arm, but, little by little, she managed it. She was nearly halfway to the surface when twin beams of light crested the edge of the hole and found her clinging to the crumbling dirt wall. A warm relief surged through her as the beams settled on her upturned face. The glare was blinding, but she didn't mind. She opened her mouth to speak, but before she could utter a syllable, someone screamed, a child maybe, and one of the lights blinked out.

The other light held steady.

"Miss Mary Jean? That you way down there?" The woman's voice was deep and lilting, and Mary Jean had known it all her life.

"Nolla Rae!" A small laugh bubbled from her throat. She struggled up another rung.

"What in the world are you doing in that hole?" Nolla Rae asked.

"Right now I'm trying to get out," she answered, pulling herself further up the ladder.

"Can you make it all right?" Nolla Rae repositioned her flashlight to illuminate the remaining rungs.

"I'm okay on this part," Mary Jean said. "But I think I'll need a hand when I get to the top."

"You scared the bejeezus out of little Jerry Lee. He thought you was some kinda haint." She let out a low chuckle. "Cain't say as I blame him, neither. You quite a sight, coming up out of the ground like that."

"I think something's wrong," Mary Jean said. Her head and shoulders emerged from the hole, but with no more rungs to pull herself up by, she'd run out of leverage. She gripped the ladder stake with her right hand and tried to heave her stomach up past the lip of the well, but it was no use. She was stuck.

"Sugar, there's all kinds of things wrong," Nolla Rae told her. "The whole town's changed like you wouldn't believe." She shone the beam on Mary Jean's face again. "And you still bleeding, looks like." Nolla Rae set the flashlight aside, its beam now disappearing into the ruined canopy of the fallen black walnut tree. "But first things first," she said and abruptly grabbed Mary Jean by her bad arm and dragged her up out of the well. Mary Jean cried out as her shoulder popped loudly.

Nolla Rae released her arm and picked up the flashlight. "Lord, girl, what did I just do?" she asked, scanning Mary Jean with the light.

Mary Jean lay still and braced herself for more pain, but none came, not like she expected. She sat up in the dirt and tentatively moved her arm. It felt better.

"I don't know," she said. "There was something wrong with my shoulder, but I think it's fixed now."

Nolla Rae touched the shoulder gently. "Well, don't say nothing to your daddy," she laughed. "He'll say I'm practicing without a license."

Mary Jean looked at the darkness around her. The landscape here wasn't much brighter than the bottom of the well. The black walnut lay shattered only a few feet away, but she couldn't even distinguish the trunk from the branches. Low clouds obscured the moon and stars, and no lights came from the town or any of the neighborhoods nearby. The only other light she saw was the bouncing beam from Jerry Lee's flashlight, seventy yards further up the gravel road. He was probably heading for the swing on his mother's porch—assuming the swing and the porch were still there.

"Is your house. . ." she began, and stopped.

"The twister passed us by," said Nolla Rae, "which is more than most folks can say tonight."

Nolla Rae's house was old and small—a three-room, tar paper shack with no electricity or plumbing, and no heat but a cookstove in the kitchen. But it had the advantage of being tucked below a sheer outcropping of rock near the top of the hill, so it was always protected from any severe weather that came in from the north. Mary Jean had played at that house as a child, climbing on the mountain of tires in the front yard and on the tin roof of the chicken coop in the back. Nolla Rae had been her babysitter, the one who'd watched over her when her mother had gone off to shop or to play bridge or golf. It seemed she had spent half her childhood on the rickety porch where Jerry Lee might now be waiting, and when her father had asked where she wanted her own house to be built, she'd chosen this spot simply because it was close to Nolla Rae's.

She never told her father that, of course, because he'd have found her reasons too sentimental. Besides, he was happy with her choice for reasons of his own—the land was cheap, for one thing, and it was only four blocks from the town square, which meant she wouldn't need an automobile.

"I'm sorry for what happened to your place," Nolla Rae

offered. "But at least you didn't lose the foundation. I bet it won't take but a week for those boys to get that frame back up again."

Mary Jean got carefully to her feet and steadied herself against one of the arching limbs of the black walnut.

"Mr. Gatlin?" she called. "Are you here?"

"Nobody here but us," said Nolla Rae, but there was an uncertainty in her words.

"He was with me when the tornado hit," said Mary Jean. "He's the one put me in the well."

Nolla Rae lowered her voice to a whisper. "You mean Mr. Gatlin with the bad leg?"

"Yes, ma'am. I'm worried he might be hurt." She took the flashlight from Nolla Rae and began to shine it through the tangle of broken branches. "He could be caught up under some of these tree limbs," she said. She bent a fan-shaped branch aside and ran the flashlight beam along the length of the split trunk. But there was no sign of Mr. Gatlin.

Nolla Rae put an arm around Mary Jean's shoulder and pulled her gently away from the fallen tree, away from the well. "Oh, sugar," she said. "They was talking about Mr. Gatlin in town this evening. They say the twister got him."

Mary Jean felt the flashlight slip through her fingers, watched the beam dance across her ravaged yard and then wink out. Her stomach dropped, and for a moment she thought she might faint again. Nolla Rae kept a firm grip on her shoulder, holding her upright, but the dizziness from the floor of the well returned, swamping her in nausea.

Nolla Rae spoke again, but Mary Jean's mind was too far away now, and though the words reached her, they arrived empty of meaning, a jumble of useless sounds, with nothing to offer but the single cold reminder that, even with Nolla Rae's kind hands keeping her steady, she was alone on a narrow and thorny path. She began to shiver uncontrollably.

And now she felt herself being led away, up the long, dark hill toward Nolla Rae's house, but that was no comfort anymore, not if a man were dead because of her. Poor Mr. Gatlin, who had told her they shouldn't be out in the storm. So why hadn't she listened? Why did she always stiffen inside when anyone told her what she ought to do? What was wrong with her, that having her own way meant more than doing what was smart, or safe, or right?

It was a part of her she despised, and yet she seemed unable to change it. Nolla Rae had told her once that she'd dug in her heels the day she was born, and Mary Jean knew it was true, that she had lived her life with her head lowered, ready to ram forward under almost any circumstance, ignoring every warning. But why? What had made her such a misfit, permanently at odds with the world around her? Why had she grown up so resentful of her father's rules, of his attitudes, of his smothering attention to her life? And where was her mother in all this, other than passed out in the bedroom from her fifth gin and tonic?

And why did she resent this baby inside her, whose very existence, she knew, was her own willful doing? Why did she resent her teachers from high school, and everyone at Mary Baldwin College, and the workmen hammering on her house, and poor Mr. Gatlin, for whom she felt inexpressible sorrow, and even Bobby, whom she'd manipulated so easily into impregnating her before he shipped out, God help her, and why, why on earth would she have done that, why trap herself into a life of changing diapers and waiting silently, angrily, for her husband to come home, as her mother had done, merely to find fault, as she knew she would, when he arrived every evening from the hardware store, tired and inattentive, and to argue with him over which movies to see, or what brand of toothpaste or cereal to buy, or what color of paint belonged on the living room walls, things that should carry no weight for people in love, but things they would succumb to anyway, and now she saw that even if Bobby did come safely home from the war, he would soon tire of the selfishness she'd inherited from her parents, he would stop loving her, which would crack her heart into more pieces than she could put together again, and they'd both be miserable, locked in a life of petty bickering, and the baby screaming in its bassinet, and laundry piling on the floor, and dishes stinking in the sink, and yet this marriage, this union she was plummeting toward, as bleak and strangled as it might turn out to be, was still what she prayed for, night and day, because even a lifetime of small disappointments would be better than the alternative, if the alternative kept Bobby from ever coming home at all, which was a possibility that grew larger each day, she understood that now, even though she'd hidden from it for weeks, from the paralyzing fear that he was already dead, telling herself the flimsiest of lies, that there could be problems with the post office, that his daily letters home had stopped because of some unforeseeable breakdown in the army's delivery system, that sacks of mail had somehow tumbled from the boat or plane and drifted now in the aimless currents of the ocean's dark bottom.

The pain in her abdomen began to build again.

"Watch your step now, sugar," Nolla Rae said softly as she helped her up onto the porch. "Mr. Statten's asleep inside—he's got an early day tomorrow—so you best stay out here."

Mary Jean looked around. Jerry Lee sat with his flashlight on the slatted porch swing, his knees drawn up to his chest, watching her intently. He focused the beam on her face.

"I'll fetch you out a blanket for that chill," Nolla Rae went on.

Mary Jean realized her teeth were chattering. Goosebumps had risen along the backs of her arms.

"Thank you," she said. She squinted into the light and tried to smile. "Jerry Lee, I think I need to sit down. You mind if I join you on that swing?"

She couldn't make out his face, but she could see that he wasn't moving.

"Boy, I'll jerk a knot in you," Nolla Rae hissed, and he scooted sideways to make room. "Now, Jerry Lee, you be nice to Miss McKinney. There's nothing to be afraid of. And quit shining that light in her face. That's not polite."

"She got blood," he said, his voice small and wavering.

"That's 'cause she hurt herself. Now you hush."

Nolla Rae stared at the boy until he sighed and switched off the light. Then she stepped quietly into the house, taking care not to let the screen door clack shut behind her. Mary Jean settled herself carefully onto the swing. The cramp was knotting more tightly now, but the pain was still manageable. She knew if she moaned or cried out it would frighten Jerry Lee, so she tried to shift her mind to something else.

"How old are you now?" she asked.

"Seven," he told her.

"I remember when you were just a baby," she said. "I used to visit your mama a lot when I was younger."

He had nothing to say to that, so she tried again.

"I'm not a haint," she said. But she heard the strain in her voice.

"Daddy says we don't believe in haints," he told her. He shifted away from her, cramming himself against the armrest, and the swing wobbled on its chain.

"You don't sound convinced," she teased. "What's your mama say?"

"She says she knows what she knows."

Mary Jean touched her hand to her face. Her cheek and her forehead were crusted with blood, or dirt, or maybe both. "I must look a sight," she said.

Then the cramp hit her in earnest. She gritted her teeth and shut her eyes tight, but the pain was too much for her. She snorted out a few short, wheezing breaths.

"You breathe like Rufus," Jerry Lee said.

She almost laughed. Rufus was an old stray in the neighborhood who'd been ransacking Nolla Rae's garbage cans for as long as she could remember. She'd once come close enough to touch his tail. She opened her eyes again.

Nolla Rae emerged quietly from the house with a blanket folded over one arm and her hands cupped around a small mixing bowl. She set the bowl carefully on the swing and then wrapped Mary Jean's shoulders in the blanket. The wool felt scratchy on her skin, but she was glad for the kindness.

"I'm sorry we got no hot water," Nolla Rae said as she drew a white washrag from the bowl and wrung it out. "But cold's better anyway if you're bleeding." She blotted the rag against the side of Mary Jean's face.

"Hurts," Mary Jean managed to say.

"I know it, sugar, but we cain't leave a scrape this dirty."

"No, my stomach." She clenched her jaw and clutched the wooden arm of the swing. "Oh, God, it hurts," she said, her voice tightening to a whine. Jerry Lee scrambled to the porch and ran inside the house. Water sloshed from the bowl as the swing bounced in its chains.

"What kind of pain?" Nolla Rae asked, but the wave was cresting now, and Mary Jean couldn't sort out an answer. Nolla Rae put her hand on Mary Jean's brow. "Is it cramps, or something else?"

"Worse," Mary Jean said, and a sob escaped her. "Like I ate poison."

Nolla Rae let out a sigh. She draped the washrag over the arm of the swing, then moved the water bowl to the porch floor and eased herself down beside Mary Jean. "Just ride it out," she said. "We'll talk when it passes."

Mary Jean wanted to argue. What if it didn't pass? She'd had egg and olive sandwiches for lunch—maybe the mayonnaise had been bad. Or what if she'd somehow got into rat poison, like strychnine or arsenic? Or drain cleaner? Most people kept that stuff around, and accidents did happen. But in the half second it took for these fears to form, the pain somersaulted forward through every nerve in her body, and all she could do was wail hoarsely across the darkened porch. She dug her fingernails into her palms to try to distract herself, but it was no use; the pain now swallowed her whole—it was a wolf, a giant snake, a whale, and she was caught inside it.

And then it eased up. Calmed down. Melted away into the soft, cool corners of the yard. Her breath came more evenly, and she was herself again. She pulled the blanket close around her and cried quietly with relief.

"You still poisoned?" Nolla Rae asked.

Mary Jean shook her head.

"I didn't think so." She folded her arms across her breasts and tapped her foot methodically on a loose board. "Was this the first time?"

Mary Jean sniffed and wiped her nose on her sleeve. "No, ma'am. The first was a while ago, when I was down in the well."

"You know what it is, don't you?"

Mary Jean shook her head again, more vigorously this time. "It can't be that. Daddy says I'm not due for another three weeks."

Nolla Rae snorted and rocked back in the swing. "Yeah, doctors like timetables. But sometimes a woman's body got plans of its own."

Mary Jean didn't know what to say to that. They sat in silence for a full minute, Nolla Rae easing the swing back and forth with her foot while Mary Jean picked up the washcloth and gingerly dabbed at the remaining blood on her face.

"It'll come back, won't it?" Mary Jean finally asked.

"Like a railroad train," Nolla Rae said. "And you tied to the tracks."

"What should I do?"

"Pick yourself a spot to have it," she said. "That's about all the choice you got left."

"Then I need to go to the hospital," Mary Jean told her.

"That's a spot," Nolla Rae agreed.

"Can you drive me there?"

Nolla Rae shrugged. "Got no automobile."

"Can't we call an ambulance?"

"Storm took out the power lines," she said. "But it wouldn't

matter anyway. Every street in town's tore up. Cain't get half a
block without finding somebody's roof in the road."

"Then I'll walk," she said, abruptly pushing herself up from
the swing. She dropped the washrag into the bowl and walked,
unsteadily, to the front of the porch. If she really were about to
have her baby, she wanted to be somewhere safe, somewhere
with bright lights and wide, clean hallways. A place with doctors
and nurses to take care of anything that might go wrong. And
ether for the pain. She pulled the blanket from her shoulders
and tried to hang it across the porch rail, but it slid to the floor.

"You in no condition," said Nolla Rae. She rose from the swing
and pulled open the screen door. "Jerry Lee," she said softly, "come
out here."

The boy emerged from the doorway and stood silently
before his mother. She leaned over and touched her head to
his. "I want you to run around back of the house and fetch me
Daddy's wheelbarrow."

The boy stepped away from her. "There's. . .things back
there," he said. "I hear 'em sometimes."

"Just clap your hands," she told him. "That'll scare all the bad
things away. You can sing, too, if you want. Now hurry up and do
what I said."

Jerry Lee walked past Mary Jean with his head down and then
disappeared quickly around the side of the house, furiously clapping
his hands. "Jesus loves the little children," he sang, his reedy voice
fading into the night air. "All the children of the world. . ."

Mary Jean gripped the support post and leaned her weight
against it. Nolla Rae was right; she'd never make it to the hospital on her own. But she wasn't crazy, either.

"Nolla Rae, I don't think a wheelbarrow is such a good
idea," she said. "Besides, I couldn't ask Mr. Statten to do a thing
like that."

"Mr. Statten's not available," Nolla Rae said curtly. "I'll be
taking you myself."

A loud clatter came from somewhere behind the house.

Mary Jean hardly knew what to say. A wheelbarrow? How
was that even possible? The hospital was out by the fairgrounds,
clear on the other side of town—nine or ten blocks away. She'd
never used a wheelbarrow herself, so she wasn't too clear on
how easily they operated, but surely Nolla Rae couldn't haul
her all the way there without help.

Nolla Rae seemed to read her thoughts. "It's all downhill," she said. "Won't be a problem at all."

Jerry Lee rounded the corner of the house, awkwardly guiding the wheelbarrow ahead of him.

"It had bricks," he said. "I had to tump it over."

"That's a good boy," Nolla Rae told him. "I'll give you a penny when I get home."

"I scared the bad things away," he said.

The screen door banged open, and Mr. Statten stepped out onto the porch. Mary Jean couldn't make out his face in the darkness, but from his movements she guessed he was pulling his suspenders up over his shoulders.

"What's all the racket out here?" he demanded. "Nolla Rae, you know I got to go to Huntsville in the morning."

"Mary Jean McKinney's done gone into labor," Nolla Rae explained. "I'm borrowing your wheelbarrow to take her to the hospital."

Mr. Statten took a step toward Mary Jean and looked into her face, then at her swollen belly, then at the wheelbarrow, which Jerry Lee had propped beside the porch step.

"Awright, then," he said, "but this young'un ought to be in bed." He turned and went back into the house.

"You heard your daddy," said Nolla Rae, and Jerry Lee followed his father into the house. "Now you," she said, turning to Mary Jean, "get in the wheelbarrow. We need to cover some ground before the next contraction."

Mary Jean stepped down into the yard. "How. . .?"

"I'll tip it forward," she said. "You just cradle into it, and lean back."

Mary Jean did as she was told, and Nolla Rae wheeled her from the yard to the street. Gravel popped beneath the tire as they wobbled their way ridiculously down the slope. On any day of her childhood, she would have thought it fun to ride like this through the night. But childhood was over now. Her new house had vanished in a puff of wind. Mr. Gatlin was dead. The baby was coming too soon, tearing her body apart. And Bobby was missing in Korea.

She started to say something to Nolla Rae, something trivial, about Rufus the dog, or haints, or bricks in the backyard— anything to keep a conversation going, anything to keep herself distracted.

But she changed her mind. Sometimes it was better not to talk. Bobby was lost somewhere in the war, and talking was a waste of breath.

But he'd come home soon; he had to. She needed him—she saw that now—really needed him, clear down to her bones. She'd never told him that, but she would, first thing, and then he'd smile and scoop her up and pull this rusty knife blade from her heart.

For now, though, she needed to focus. She needed to prepare herself. She needed to greet the next pain differently, whenever it arrived.

HISTORY LESSONS

Things took a turn for me over breakfast at Bill's Pool Hall Cafe, waiting for Dell to pick me up for the morning repo run. Bill had just served me a plate of bacon and grits and was starting on his first load of dishes from the daylight rush. There were still a few Tuesday-nighters playing poker at a table near the back, but otherwise the place was empty, which was typical for the time of day. Summer mornings, Bill's is pretty crowded from dawn to about seven-thirty, when the old truck farmers gather to drink coffee and speculate about the weather. They leave their dusty pickups lined up outside against the courthouse lawn in that first long shade of the day, clotting the south side of the square with half-loads of peanuts and sweet corn, snap beans and yellow squash, peaches and cantaloupes, cucumbers and tomatoes, watermelons and yams. I've loved the sight of that all my life. But anyway, by eight o'clock the truck farmers have finished their coffee and moved across the street to the stone benches around the monument to the local Confederate dead, leaving Bill's place empty except for a few late starters like me and whatever pool hustlers or card players might be left over from the night before.

Bill left the first load of dishes to soak and moved down toward my end of the counter, smearing his gray rag across the countertop along the way, pausing here and there to scrub up a spill stain or a spot of dried egg. He guided the rag around my plate and pushed the pile of crumbs over the edge of the counter onto the dark wooden floor. A fat housefly buzzed casually between us, and Bill waved it away with a single slow sweep of his hand. "How's the chow this morning?" he asked.

"Greasy," I told him. "You barely got the chill off this bacon." Bill's a nice fellow, but he's kind of erratic as a cook because he almost never cleans his grill and he treats every hot order like he's just warming up leftovers. Still, I like it here. There's always that thick, fresh smell of breakfast in the air. It's funny, but in the long run, I can get more comfort out of the way food smells than the way it tastes. Taste swallows itself away in a minute or two, but a good smell can hang in the mind forever. Of course, so can a bad one.

Bill shrugged and looked past me to the table of poker players. "Hey, Morgan," he called, "I got another gripe about the food. Maybe you oughta investigate." Morgan Motlow is a health inspector with the state, but he was born and raised here in the county so the only places he ever cites for health violations are the fast food franchises out on the highway. He runs the regular Tuesday night game; nobody sits in without Morgan's say-so.

He tipped his chair back and squinted toward us. The sun was high enough now to set up a glare through the front windows, so I guess he had trouble making us out. Or maybe he was a little drunk—there were three pint bags on the floor beside his chair. "Is that you, Junior?" he said. Morgan grew up with both my parents, and even though I'm not named after my father, he's called me Junior all my life. I could tell by the tone of his voice he'd had a lucky night.

"Yeah, Morgan, it's me."

"Well, how the hell are you, boy? Ain't seen you since Hector was a pup." He looked back down at his cards and slid a small stack of chips to the center of the table. The other four players all threw in their hands, and Morgan broke into a loud cackle. "You dumb sons of bitches," he said. He had to be drunk. I knew a couple of the other players in the game— Buddy Pilot and Ricky Malone were two or three years older than me, but we'd all been in eighth grade together, and they'd been dangerous even then. They weren't the kind of fellows any sober man would laugh at.

Bill shook out his rag and draped it over the side of the sink. "Nolan says the bacon's greasy. Says you ought to close me down. Put me out on the street so I can get me some of them welfare checks."

"Hell, bacon's supposed to be greasy," Morgan said, raking the pot into his pile of chips. "Dish him up another bowl of grits. Grits'll soak up anything."

"No, thanks," I said before Bill could even offer. I'm not a picky eater, but you could patch a driveway with Bill's leftover grits.

Buddy Pilot suddenly stood up from the table. "I gotta piss," he said, "but deal me in anyway, I'm coming right back." He swayed a little in place, looking around the room like he didn't know where he was. Then his eyes focused on the restroom door and he tilted straight for it, ramming several chairs and tables along the way.

I turned back to the remainder of my breakfast. Bill was trying to scrape the last of the cold grits into the garbage pail beneath the counter.

"Looks like a long game," I said.

Bill glanced past me to the poker table. "Too long. I wish they'd break it up and go home." He began to work the spoon edge against the inside of the bowl like he was whittling a knot-hole out of a stick. When he'd gouged away all he could, he eased the bowl into the sudsy dishwater and picked up his old Timex from the back of the sink. He studied the watch face for a moment, then held it out toward me. "What time does it say?"

"Ten after eight," I told him.

He squinted out through the front plate-glass window. "Well, if Marty don't show up soon, he can kiss this job goodbye. I'm too old to be staying up all night and then work his shift, too." He frowned. "Hey, somebody told me you don't sell insurance no more."

"That's right," I said.

"If you're looking for work, I think Marty's about to leave a vacancy."

"Thanks," I said, "but I've already signed on with Hometown Finance."

Bill rummaged through the dark water and pulled up several paring knives, which he rinsed briefly under the tap. "You'd be better off washing dishes," he said, dropping the knives onto the drainer.

I knew what he meant. When you work for the finance company, there's paperwork and neckties and a dozen other things to make it seem like a real office job, but the gist of it all is to be the bad news on somebody's doorstep, and that's a sad career for anybody.

It crossed my mind to tell him about finding Jerry Moffit on Monday's repo run, but that would've got Dell involved, and he was already mad at me for making him report the body, even though he hung up when the dispatcher asked for his name. Dell figures that whatever happens on the job is our business and nobody else's. Maybe he's right, maybe privacy is the least we can offer. Doctors, lawyers, preachers, undertakers—they're all supposed to keep the details quiet. Maybe repo men are, too.

Just then the front door creaked open, jiggling the tiny bell above the frame, and Bill and I both turned to see who it was, both of us, I suppose, expecting it to be Marty. No such luck. From where I sat the morning glare was at its worst, almost blinding, reflecting in from the bright chrome trim of the trucks across the square. But even through that white wall of haze it wasn't hard for me to recognize the tidy silhouette of my father.

I suppose he must have spotted me, too, because he paused in the doorway like he had second thoughts about coming inside. We hadn't spoken in more than a month, not since he'd fired me from the agency, so I really didn't know exactly how things stood between us. I wasn't even sure I wanted to find out. He took a seat at the counter four stools down, just far enough away to make conversation optional.

Bill lifted the coffeepot from the warmer and fished out a clean cup from beneath the counter. "Well, look who's here," he said, smiling. Just about everybody smiles at my father; by now he must think it's the most natural expression on the human face. Bill filled the cup to the brim, still smiling, and eased it across the worn Formica. "What can I get for you today, Jimmy?"

My father brushed some imaginary crumbs from the counter and leaned forward onto his forearms. His limp gray suit was wrinkled and sweat-stained, as it always was by midweek. "What have you got that's good?" he asked, keeping his eyes focused on the wall above the fry vat like he thought there was a menu there.

"Not much if you listen to Nolan," Bill told him. "The boy thinks I'm trying to clog his arteries."

I plucked the Wednesday edition of the *Observer* from where the previous customer had left it wedged between two napkin dispensers, and pretended to read the front page. But then I noticed Jerry Moffit was the lead story, and I stopped pretending. The coroner said natural causes, which probably surprised a lot of people, given Jerry's notoriety. A bullet or an overdose would have seemed more normal, or even a bashed-in skull. If he'd been stabbed to death by a church deacon in some smokey rented room on some hot Saturday night, nobody would have thought it odd. But all he did was sit down in a chair and die, which was the one thing nobody would have expected. They ran an old photo of Jerry next to the article, one of him in his uniform. Private Jerald Moffit: dopey grin, panicky eyes, hair that looked scraggly even in a crew cut. I never knew Jerry well, but I did know some of his old pals. They said he was a normal guy until Vietnam.

Ricky Malone let out a holler from the back of the room. "Buddy, get your sorry ass out here," he called. "We're dealing the hand."

I glanced around in time to see him hurl an empty pint bottle across the room at the restroom door. It was plastic and bounced away into a corner.

"Here, now," Bill said. "We'll have none of that."

I could tell from his attitude that Ricky was having a good game, which was fortunate all around. I used to play cards with him myself, years back, before I realized the kind of risk I was running. Ricky gets impatient when he wins, like he thinks there's some kind of time limit on his luck. When he loses, he just turns cold. I've seen that happen, too. His face takes on an empty look, the kind you might see on a roadkill dog. Those are the looks to worry about, because you never know what they might lead to.

"I'll just have the coffee," my father said, tearing open a pair of sugar packets. "Can't afford much restaurant food—I work for a living."

"Yeah, we're a real pricy place, all right," Bill told him. "I oughta have me a mansion and a speedboat."

"Bill, give the poor man a doughnut," I said. "Put it on my ticket."

My father looked at me like I was a picture from his high school yearbook he could only vaguely recollect. Then he nodded. "Make it corn flakes, Bill. Might as well take advantage of my wealthy relatives." Bill put a small unopened box of cereal into a bowl and set it on the counter with a half-pint carton of milk, then returned his attention to the sink-full of dirty dishes. My father stirred his coffee and took a careful sip. "I hear I'm in line to be a grandfather," he said.

That was nothing I wanted to go into, which he probably guessed. Laney and I shared a certain territory—ten years of

marriage will do that much, even for the worst couples—but
we were like goalposts at the opposite ends of a field. We hadn't
yet said two words about her baby, or about her taking up with
Steve Pitts, or about when, exactly, she'd be moving out. More
items on my list of things to do.

"I wouldn't go shopping for any baby rattles just yet," I told
him. I folded the newspaper and tucked it back between the
napkin holders for the next customer.

"Kids are a big responsibility," he informed me.

"Thanks for the tip," I said. "I'll be sure to pass it along." I
don't think he understood what I was telling him—which was
fine. In any case, I knew he wouldn't press it further, not without
encouragement from me. My father is not the sort of talker who
can hold up two ends of a conversation. Or even one. For him,
talking is more or less a tool of the trade, a way to sell insurance.
Outside of that, he rarely knows what to say.

Except, of course, when he fired me. He knew exactly what
to say then: "Nolan, you're fired." It was a real breakthrough
for him.

And the truth is, I was happy not to have to listen to all the
reasons. I was a crappy insurance salesman, I already knew that.
Still, what kind of man fires his own son?

The restroom door swung open, banging hard against the
wall, and Buddy Pilot came ambling back into the room, still
zipping up his fly. "What's the game?" he asked.

"Seven card stud," Ricky told him. "You're two rounds behind,
but we made your bets for you. You raised us on the second
round."

Buddy lowered himself into his chair. "What have I got?" he
asked.

Morgan scrutinized the up-cards spread across the table.
"From the look of it, not a goddamn thing," he said. "We all
figure you're bluffing."

My father scowled toward the poker table. "There's sure no
shortage of deadbeats in this town," he said. "I guess you got
some job security after all."

"It's steady enough work," I told him.

He took another sip of his coffee and tore open the box of
corn flakes. "So how come you're sitting here on a work day?
Bill, I hope you don't owe this bloodsucker any money. Better
watch your toaster if you do."

"I'm waiting for Dell," I explained. "We use his truck for pickups."

Bill wiped his hands on his apron and shook his head. "If you're waiting for Dell, you just got yourself a day off," he said. "Dell spent the night right over there." He nodded toward the poker game. "Went home about an hour ago, broke as a dead branch. You just missed him."

My father poured coffee over his corn flakes and reached for more sugar packets. "I guess the work's not as steady as you thought."

"I can live with the disappointment," I told him, though in fact I did hate to lose the money. Dell was on salary with Hometown Finance so it didn't matter if he laid off a day, but I was just an under-the-table jobber. They didn't carry me on their regular payroll.

My father scooped up a spoonful of the corn flakes I'd bought him and held them steady over the bowl, studying them through his bifocals. "What the hell's wrong with these flakes?" he asked.

"You put coffee on them instead of milk," I told him.

Bill chuckled. "And here I thought you was just being exotic," he said.

My father lowered the spoon back into the bowl. He'd made a few other mistakes like that lately—not many, and never anything big, but they were starting to add up. He pushed the bowl away from him and wiped his mouth with his napkin like he'd just finished a big meal. "I'm too damn old," he said.

Bill snapped his fingers. "That reminds me." He took a clipboard from the wall above the butcher's block. "Before you go slopping any more coffee on my counter, sign this petition."

Bill handed the clipboard to my father, who squinted down his nose at the top sheet of paper. "What's it for?" he asked.

Bill leaned across the counter and tapped his finger on the paper. "I'm trying to get the state historical society to register this place as a landmark."

My father took a pen from his shirt pocket and signed his name to the list. "Why do you want it registered?" he asked.

"So I can get a tax break when I have to put on a new roof next year," Bill told him.

"What's so historical about this place?" I asked.

Bill looked annoyed. "Didn't they teach you anything in school? In 1902, Frank James shot a man dead right here in this room."

I looked around the cafe, expecting, I guess, to see something significant, something I'd never noticed before. But it was the same worn-down place as always. No bullet holes in the tin ceiling tiles, no blood stains on the checkered tablecloths, no ghost of Frank James loitering by the door. Just the same three rickety pool tables, the same yellow lacquered walls, the same pair of ancient ceiling fans clicking slowly overhead.

"How do you know it's true?" I asked.

Bill took the clipboard from my father and passed it to me. "Everybody knows it," he said. "It's common knowledge."

I signed my name below my father's. Even his handwriting looked old, full of sharp angles and tiny tremors. "What'd he shoot him for?" I asked.

"Hell, I don't know," Bill said, taking back his petition. "I guess the guy just pissed him off."

My father suddenly swiveled his stool in my direction and smiled. "I've got an idea," he said. "I could do with a day off myself. How about you and me take a trip down to Horseshoe Bend. Tour the battlefield. See some real historical landmarks."

"That's a five-hour drive," I said.

I don't know what it is with my father and war memorials. When I was a kid, every family vacation, every weekend trip, even every Sunday afternoon drive took us to some kind of military park or battleground. I've eaten picnic lunches on the gravestones at Shiloh, Antietam, Chickamauga, Bull Run, Stones River, Cold Harbor, Kennesaw Mountain, Gettysburg, and a dozen other Civil War crossroads. I've stood where George Washington stood at Yorktown, where Campbell stood at King's Mountain, Morgan at the Cowpens, Greene at Guilford Courthouse. I've seen the view Andrew Jackson had when he fought the Muskogee at Talladega, at Emuckfa, and at Enotochopko Creek. I've hacked through the overgrowth where Red Eagle led the massacre at Fort Mims, and I've walked the wooded ridge at Tippecanoe. At my father's relentless insistence, I've read the inscriptions on a hundred small-town courthouse monuments honoring the dead from at least a dozen wars. I've stood before countless roadside markers commemorating where some distinguished troop of soldiers once set up camp, or stopped a retreat, or came down with fever, or rested, or surrendered, or died. I've climbed Creek burial mounds, and I've even paid my respects at the Fentress County homestead of

Sergeant Alvin York, the conscientious objector who won the Medal of Honor. But in all our travels the Horseshoe Bend on the Tallapoosa River had inexplicably escaped our list.

My father started to say something more—some argument, I suppose, in favor of the trip—but a sudden commotion at the poker table cut him off. We both turned in time to see Buddy Pilot fling his chair aside and drag the big table awkwardly toward him. When he'd pulled it clear of the other players, he flipped it over, scattering cards and chips across the floor. "You rigged it!" he shouted. "You rigged it while I was gone!"

The other players seemed too surprised to react, and for a few long seconds Buddy just stood there, fists clenched, daring anybody to stand. But nobody did—they just stared back at him, calm but interested, like he was a carnival sideshow act. Finally, Morgan leaned forward in his chair. "So what's your point?" he said, and everybody but Buddy started to laugh. Buddy might have done something then—he was mad enough—but by that time Bill had come up beside him. Bill's a pretty old guy, over seventy, but he was a marine MP in the South Pacific, and he still knows how to handle himself. He stuck his leg behind Buddy to trip him, then grabbed him by the scruff of his shirt collar and jerked him straight over backwards. Buddy hit the floor hard and vomited all over himself. I guess we all winced at that, and a couple of the other players edged their chairs away to make room for whatever Buddy might try when he got up; but he didn't get up, he just lay there on his back, groaning.

Bill leaned down across him and shook a finger in his face. "Don't treat my furniture like that," he said. Buddy gurgled something, and then Bill hoisted him up by his belt buckle and walked him to the back door. "Now go home," he said, shoving him gently through the doorway into the alley. Then he walked back to his stack of dirty dishes, giving Morgan a hard look along the way.

Morgan stood up and stretched. "Y'all clean up this mess," he said. "And watch how you divvy up those chips—I know what I had in front of me." Ricky Malone muttered something I didn't catch, but for once he did what he was told, getting down on his hands and knees to rake the chips together into a pile. He dropped the first handful noisily into the battered Christmas cookie tin Bill used for their storage.

"The hell with this," one of the other two said. "Ain't none of my money on that floor." As he stood and headed for the door, I got my first clear look at him. He was short and skinny with a pockmarked face, and it seemed to me I'd maybe seen him operating one of the carnival rides at the county fair. The Tilt-a-Whirl, or the Scrambler. I don't think he was local.

Morgan didn't waste any breath calling him back but turned to the other one I didn't know, a pale-looking, moon-faced man in a blue checkered shirt. "What about it, Rolly?" he asked.

Rolly rubbed the side of his face and frowned toward the door. "Yeah, okay," he said. He squatted in front of his chair and began to gather up the mingled decks of cards.

Morgan stepped around the overturned table and joined us at the counter. "Still just a bunch of kids," he said, shaking his head.

But he was wrong. I don't know the story on Rolly or the carnival guy, but Buddy and Ricky had never been kids, not for as long as I'd known them. Although I couldn't say why. Their parents are all decent, well-to-do people—Ricky's dad owns a furniture store just off the square, and Buddy's folks have a good-sized farm south of town. I've sat with both families at church picnics, Little League games, and Lions Club bingo. On the surface of it, there's just no reason why Ricky or Buddy should be any meaner or wilder than anybody else. But they are.

Maybe they got bad treatment somewhere along the line—a lot of people think that's how it works, that we only turn out bad if bad things get done to us first. But I don't think that's the whole answer. When a lizard or a snake first cracks out of its shell, it already knows what to do in the world, and it won't ever change. Maybe some of us are more like that, born with something we can't ever get rid of, some basic knowledge that right away makes us who we are.

Morgan eased himself onto one of the stools between my father and me. Bill handed him a roll of paper towels and a spray bottle of cleaner. "We can't be having any more of this, Morgan," he said. "You gotta keep these pups in line."

Morgan whistled toward the back and tossed the paper towels and the cleaner to Rolly. "Spic and span," he ordered, "like it was your own mama's kitchen." Then he leaned his elbows on the counter and ran his fat hands up over his freckled scalp, smoothing down what was left of his hair. "What those boys need is a hitch in the army," he said.

"Amen to that," Bill agreed. "Worst thing ever happened to this country was they got rid of the draft."

"Don't know if I can agree with that," I said, thinking about how people like Jerry Moffit might have turned out differently if they hadn't been put through a war.

"'Course you don't agree with it," said Morgan, pressing the heels of his hands to his eyes. "You never been in the service." Morgan was an infantryman who'd been on Iwo Jima and at Guadalcanal.

"The service is good training for anybody," Bill said. He pointed to a framed piece of paper on the wall above the grill, but it was so blotted with grease I couldn't tell what it was. "The Marines is where I first learned to cook," he went on. "And after that they even taught me judo."

"Well, that makes sense," said Morgan. "The way you cook, self-defense was the next logical step." He started to laugh, but it turned into a deep, wheezing cough that took him nearly a minute to bring under control. When the fit finally passed, he wiped the water from his eyes with a napkin and took a few slow, rattling breaths. "But Bill's right, Junior," he said at last. "The service can help anybody along." His voice was hoarse now, but more urgent, as if the emphysema had reminded him he was running out of words. He turned to my father. "Jimmy, you need to take this boy in hand," he chided. "Let him know what's what. Explain the virtues of the military life."

"Too late now," my father said. "He's old and he's fat."

"Nothing wrong with fat," said Bill. "Fat means officer material." His grin stretched wide, and his gold tooth flashed in the sun.

Morgan shook his head. "These punks today—they think the army's just some kind of hard-ass summer camp where you have to get up early and clean toilets. They ain't got a goddamn clue." He turned to me. "Junior, your daddy was a bombardier in the Army Air Corps, in case you didn't know it."

"Yeah, I know it," I said. "He was on a B-24." I said this like I was some kind of expert on my father's military career. In fact, I knew almost nothing about it. I'd heard a little bit from relatives who didn't know much themselves, and that was about it. The war was something my father didn't normally talk about, at least not around me. In my twenty-eight years I'd heard him bring it up only once, when I was about twelve. We were in a dime store together, and I was looking at all the plastic model kits of World War II planes. He pointed to the green picture of the B-24 box and said it was the kind of plane he had flown. I even remember thinking that was a good thing for me to know. But I bought the B-29 instead because it had more guns.

"He flew thirty-five missions over Germany," Morgan went on, "and believe me, he *got* something out of all that."

"All I got out of the service was a sweet tooth," my father said. "Never cared much for sweets before I went in, I guess because my mother used to mix in sugar with the cod-liver oil she gave me when I was little." He shook his head and smiled. "She thought the sugar would make the medicine taste better. But all it did was ruin the sugar."

"So," I said, "how'd you get a sweet tooth in the Air Corps?" It was the first question I'd ever asked him about the war. He looked over at me in surprise.

"Well," he said, "they always gave us each a box of candy to take with us on a mission. English hard candy. For sustenance. Because we were gone eight or ten hours at a stretch. So you'd take off your oxygen mask and stick a piece of hard candy in there and then put your mask back on. That way you could suck on the candy and still have your oxygen."

"But tell him about the *war*," Morgan said, obviously disappointed in my father's sense of drama. "Tell him what happened. Tell him some of the things you saw."

"I didn't see much of anything," my father said. "I was up in the airplane most of the time. When you're six miles off the ground, everything looks pretty much the same. It all just flattens out, like a big map. It was you boys"— he nodded to both Bill and Morgan —"it was you boys on the ground who saw the war."

There was a pause while Morgan turned this over in his mind. He looked disturbed, as if it had never before occurred to him that someone could fight in the same war he did and not know what it looked like.

"You must have seen *something*," he insisted. "Jimmy, they gave you the DSC, for chrissakes. They don't hand those out for milk runs."

"What's the DSC?" I asked. Both Bill and Morgan looked at me in disbelief, as if I'd just asked what lungs were for, or why the sun moved across the sky. My father focused his eyes on his coffee cup, which he began to rotate between his palms, like a pot-maker working in slow motion. He seemed embarrassed, but I couldn't tell if it were for himself or for me.

"The DSC is the Distinguished Service Cross," said Morgan, a seriousness in his voice now I'd never heard before. "They give it for exceptional heroism in combat. Not just heroism, you understand, but *exceptional* heroism. The DSC is just a notch down from the Medal of Honor."

Bill picked up the coffeepot and freshened my father's cup. "Didn't you get shot down?" he asked.

My father didn't answer right away, but then he looked up and smiled. It was his hollow, insurance salesman smile, the one I'd always seen in him as a sign of retreat.

"Yeah," he said brightly. "But in most ways it turned out all right."

"Jimmy, that's not the point," said Morgan. "We know it turned out all right—you're here, for god sakes. The point is the *impression* it made on you. The good it did you. How it *affected* you."

My father looked genuinely puzzled. "I don't think it affected me much at all. I mean, I didn't get hurt or anything. It was just sort of—well—a bad day."

Bill snorted. "A bad day," he repeated. "The guy gets shot down and calls it a bad day."

"Does this go here?" Rolly called out, positioning the poker table near the rear corner.

"Yeah, that's fine," Bill told him. "Now just straighten up those chairs around it and clear away those empties."

Ricky Malone came up holding the tin of poker chips and set it on the stool beside Morgan. "Me and Rolly both cashed in already," he said. "Count yours if you like, but keep in mind we ain't giving anything back."

Morgan smiled and plucked a handful of bills from the tin. "This looks fine," he said, though he barely glanced at the wadded cash. Even I knew Ricky Malone wouldn't dare short-change him.

"Here, sign this before you go," Bill said, handing his petition back across the counter.

Ricky took the clipboard. "That Frank James thing?" He studied the sheet and then nodded. "Yeah, all right. Gimme a pen. I'd like to see a plaque up here about that." I gave him my pen and he scribbled his name in broad strokes across two signature lines. "You know," he said, sliding the clipboard across the counter, "those were wide-open times. If I'd lived back then, I coulda made a real name for myself, I guarantee it."

"Yeah, you woulda been famous, all right," said Morgan. "You woulda been the guy that Frank James shot."

Ricky gave Morgan a last cold look and sauntered toward the rear door. Bill followed after him to inspect the cleanup work.

"Good enough," Bill said as Ricky disappeared into the alley. "I'll mop up later." He slapped a dish towel across his shoulder and walked back to the sink. Rolly snatched up his baggy yellow sport coat from the back of a chair and followed Ricky outside. The rest of us sat there for a minute in the calm.

"It was our twenty-first bombing run," my father said suddenly. "I remember because it was also Danny Durbin's twenty-first birthday. Danny was our pilot. Great guy—I still get Christmas cards from him. But imagine—just twenty-one years old. And Danny was the old man on the crew, two years older than anybody else. Three years older than me."

"What was your target?" Morgan wanted to know.

The question seemed to startle him, as if he'd forgotten for a moment we were there. He took a sip of coffee and dabbed his napkin at the corners of his mouth. "Well, it's funny," he said, "but when I think about those missions, the numbers seem to stay with me more than the names. I guess that's because the numbers were my countdown for going home." He tilted his head back and thought for a moment. "But I think this one might have been the rail yards at Dresden."

Bill stopped washing the dishes. "You bombed Dresden?"

"I bombed just about everything," my father said. "Morgan had it right—thirty-five missions. He sounded almost cheerful about it, but there was a distance in his voice, too, like he wasn't really talking to us at all.

We got quiet again. I knew about the Dresden raid—not that my father had been part of it, that was news, but that it had been one of the truly terrible chapters of the war. Not even Morgan could cheerlead for the firestorm at Dresden.

"Dresden was tough luck," Bill said solemnly.

"It was a disaster, all right," my father said, though still more to himself, it seemed, than to any of us. "I've never seen such a screw-up in my life." He sat up straight on his stool and swiveled slightly toward us, smoothing his hands along the tired creases in his trousers. He looked nervous, artificially alert, like someone on the witness stand, and I could see that, for whatever reason, he had determined to speak the whole thing out, once and for all. And then, I suppose, be done with it. "There were bomber groups there from every base in England," he went on, "way too many for the size of the target zone. There wasn't space enough to hold us. But we all went in, all at once, because that's what they told us to do.

"And in all the confusion, one of the other bomber groups flew right across the top of us, and we could see the bombs falling from their planes. Hundreds and hundreds of bombs, strung out all across the sky, and us right in the middle of it. That might have been the end, right there, but Danny tipped the plane up on its side so the bombs wouldn't be as likely to hit our wings. And that saved us—we passed on through. But when he tipped us up like that, see, we couldn't get all our bombs to release, and we had one stuck halfway out the bomb-bay door. Well, we straightened up after we made our run, and started back for England. But we still had that one bomb caught in the bomb bay. It just wouldn't release.

"In the meantime, from flak we had one engine shot out and another was throwing oil, so we only had two good engines. And Danny said, 'I think maybe I can land this thing, but I don't know.' He said, 'I'm gonna give you guys your choice—you can either bail out, or you can stick with it, stick with the plane.' And we all said, 'Well, it's pretty cold out there, we'll stick with the plane.' So Danny told the planes ahead of us what the trouble was, and that we were gonna try to land somewhere back across the lines. Then they flew on to England, and we started down.

"Well, we were lucky again, because about three miles beyond the lines there was this airport—I keep thinking it was at Reims, but I'm not certain, I've forgotten the town. And we notified the little airport there about our problem, said we had a bomb that might be armed, that might go off when we landed. So just about everybody cleared the area right away. Usually, you know, there'd be crowds of people coming out to welcome you down, but this was a different situation. Only two people came out on the runway to greet us. I saw them both through the bomb-bay doors, waving up at us while we circled the field.

I found out later that one was a French prostitute; the other was a little boy who thought he might get some of our candy." My father stopped and took a swallow of coffee.

"What do you mean about not knowing if the bomb was armed?" I asked.

He shrugged. "Well, just that: we didn't know. See, the fuses on the bombs had these little propellers, and once that propeller had spun two hundred and fifty revolutions, the bomb was armed. Normally, there'd be a little wire stuck in the propeller blades to keep it from turning. The wire had a little snap on one end, and that's what you attached to the bomb bays. When the bomb dropped, naturally that pulled the wire out and the propeller would start revolving. And that would arm it on its way down.

"But what happened in this case was the front bomb shackles had released like they were supposed to, so the front part of the bomb had dropped down into the slipstream. But the rear shackles didn't release, either because they were bent or because they were frozen. So that was the problem. The bomb wasn't all the way out of the plane, but it had dropped just far enough to pull that wire out, and I could see the propeller down there, going *ching, ching, ching,* making little slow circles at the edge of the slipstream. So we just didn't know."

"That's when I woulda jumped," said Bill.

"I thought about it," my father said. "But then Danny told me I should climb down into the lower bay and try to kick the thing loose somehow. I was the bombardier, after all, besides being the youngest, so it made sense that I'd be the one to try, if anybody did. But I never imagined for a minute that it might work. Bombs are heavier than you might think. It was like trying to kick a Chevy off the side of the road. But anyway, I climbed on down, and Danny said to hurry because he couldn't keep us in the air much longer, so I started kicking at the shackles over and over. Kicked until my feet went numb, but even then I couldn't stop because I was afraid that if I did we might all blow up. So I just kept at it and kept at it and then Danny said, 'Ready or not,' and my stomach got light as the plane dropped down—we weren't positioned for the land-ing yet, but still the plane was dropping down—and I figured this was it, this was it for sure. The plane began to buck and shake, and the two good engines started to sputter. But I kept on kicking at those shackles. I shut everything else out of my mind and just kept kicking and kicking, while Danny banked us across the runway to come around for the final approach. And then I sort of heard the explosion beneath us and the cheering in the plane. But even then I didn't stop kicking. It was like nothing had registered—the bomb was gone and I didn't even know it.

"But then, of course, I did know it, and for a second I was glad, because I'd done my job. But we weren't home free, not yet, we were still going down. And now we had a different problem, because the bomb—it was the damnedest thing, but somehow I had kicked loose the bomb at the worst possible moment, and now we'd blown a hole in our own runway and set half the landing strip on fire—because these were more than just bombs, these were incendiaries. But there was no choice now. So down we went, and in we came, and the tires hit the hard-packed dirt and the ground blurred beneath me. Then Danny steered us hard to the right, out toward a field, away from the crater and the wall of fire, and I felt us tip again as I climbed up out of the bay, and the left wing scraped and banged along the ground and for a second I thought the plane might cartwheel and kill us anyway, for all our trouble. But it didn't, it just spun sideways off the runway and plowed into a field of matted weeds and frozen black dirt. Then everything was still—not quiet yet, but still, and we all knew it was over. We knew that we had—*survived*."

As he told us this last, my father's face seemed burdened with wonder, as if survival were the one thing he would never understand.

"You see?" said Morgan, turning from my father to me. "That's what I'm talking about. Putting your lives on the goddamn line together and pulling each other through—that's what the military's all about. And I don't give a good goddamn if you go on to win the lottery or get elected president, you'll never find anything that good again." His face grew red as he spoke, and for the first time I realized what a truly indelible mark the army had left on Morgan. Two teenage years in the South Pacific had made him a sergeant for life.

My father took off his glasses and polished them with his dirty napkin. "So that was it," he said. "We stayed there eight days fixing the plane. Then we flew back to England, to our home base. They gave us all medals for not being dead."

Morgan slapped the counter and laughed. "Dead? You boys were in heaven!" he said. "Eight days in a liberated town—what in hell could be sweeter than that!" He winked at me and Bill. "I think I'd like to hear a little more about that French prostitute who came out to meet you."

My father looked at him strangely, then cleared his throat. "Well, that's what I've been telling you," he said. His voice was patient and apologetic, as if he were explaining some misunderstood clause in a homeowner's policy. "The woman and the little boy were killed. It turned out I had killed them both." He waited, as if he expected some kind of reply, but Morgan didn't seem to know what to say. None of us did. Finally, when it was clear we had nothing to contribute, my father checked his watch, frowned at the time, and pushed himself up from his stool. He drew a handful of change from his pants pocket and portioned out a few coins onto the counter by his coffee cup. "Well, I'll see you boys later," he said, and walked out the door into the sunshine. He stood there for a minute on the sidewalk, watching, I guess, the farmers arranging their tomato and peach baskets on the benches across the square. He seemed, right then, to be a truly harmless man, and for the first time in a very long while, I didn't hate the sight of him.

SURVIVALISTS

John Dale rushed through the dark house to the kitchen, the wet sack in front of him, trying not to drip on the oriental rugs. Fins poked precariously through the bag in several places, and he worried that the soggy bottom might not survive even this short trip in from the car. He moved smoothly through the musty rooms, his arms locked statue-firm beneath the weight of the catch. When at last he eased the sack onto the porcelain drain beside the sink, he felt a wave of relief—the pilot touching down safely on the carrier deck.

John Dale hadn't cleaned fish in years, and he wasn't sure he still remembered how. In any case, he was glad Sheila wasn't here to watch him, to look over his shoulder while he tried to reacquaint himself with the old techniques. Even after seven years together he still found it difficult to work with her around. She had a more critical eye than anyone he'd ever known. Sometimes, when she bore down on him with her full concentration, he felt as if she were performing secret miniature autopsies on his every move.

She agreed to go with him today only to avoid being left alone in the house. John Dale had hoped that once they got to the lake she might get caught up in his enthusiasm. But she never did.

He moved to the dark wall by the kitchen doorway and found the light switch with his elbow. His hands were filthy and covered with the stink that always accompanied fishing—though he'd never figured out whether the smell came from the fish or the worms. That afternoon at least a dozen worms had burst in his grasp as he tried to hold their wriggling bodies still enough to thread the curve of the hook through their full length. And of the fish he'd caught that day—of the fish he and Sheila had caught that day—all but one had swallowed the hook, forcing him to pry their mouths apart and tear loose the tender workings of their throats.

Retrieving a swallowed hook was certainly worse than baiting one, but in fact John Dale hated to do either one. He was embarrassed with himself for feeling so squeamish, but he couldn't help it. He had confessed this to Sheila while he was baiting her hook, and regretted it at once.

"I wish you'd grow up," she told him. "It's natural to kill things. That's how we survive."

John Dale thought it over. Maybe she was right. After all, fish were certainly no high point of Creation. They didn't even have enough evolutionary development to close their eyes. And worms weren't much of anything—just rich pieces of dirt. Maybe guilt was not a proper consideration here.

He had still been weighing the pros and cons when the catfish struck his line. He raised it instantly from the murky water and swung it high up the grassy bank. Then as quickly as he could—quickly, to keep it from flopping back down to the lake—he pinned it with his foot and maneuvered his hands around the sleek, fat body, carefully avoiding the stinging fins. It was a beautiful catch, over eighteen inches long, and John Dale realized immediately that he'd landed it only by the sheerest luck. The hook was hardly in the fish at all. It dangled, blue and gleaming, from the lower lip, a slight snag only. John Dale knew that if he hadn't pulled the catfish up so swiftly, robbing it of its own reaction time, it could easily have slipped his line with almost no harm done. This fish had not been caught by skill; it had simply run afoul of a blind reflex quicker than its own.

A sudden movement in the paper sack startled John Dale into a backward spin from the sink. He stumbled against the gas heater by the pantry door.

"Jesus," he said, steadying himself against the countertop. He hadn't expected any of the fish to still be alive. They'd all been out of the water for—how long? He'd left the lake a half hour ago, at least. Then there was the time it took him to disassemble the poles and put away the tackle—and before that, in the space between the catfish and the dark, the time that he and Sheila had argued, disagreeing about dinner. So these fish had been high and dry for well over an hour, some even longer. He didn't know what the facts were in a case like this, but he'd always assumed that fish didn't get along on land any better than people did underwater. Apparently he was wrong.

He dumped the bag into the sink and looked carefully at the assortment of fish. None of them seemed to have any flop left in them now. They all looked dead. But that's the way it was with fish—even when they were still spasming on the lake bank and pumping their gills, they already looked dead. It was the only look fish knew. John Dale blamed it on their eyes.

He turned the cold water tap on full and let the stream splash down hard into the jumble of fish, thinking this might wash away some of the grass and dirt they'd picked up from the lake bank. He somehow thought they should be made clean and neat before he gutted them. What he hadn't expected was that some of the fish would be revived by the sudden blast of water. But now he counted five still moving their gills, straining for whatever refreshment the water might give. One of the two small bass was still alive, as were two bream. The catfish was still heaving, in and out, like a small lung living on its own. All the sunnies were dead.

John Dale took out an old spoon from the drawer beneath the dishrack and eased his hand down over the head of the first sunny, folding the sharp fins against the stiffening body. He had already been jabbed once by this same fish when he had tried to extract the hook from its mouth, and he wasn't about to get careless now—even a dead fish could do damage.

He could tell it was the same fish that cut him by the way he'd broken its jaw going after the hook. He'd more or less un-hinged it, and it now hung very low and crooked from the fish's face. This disfiguration gave the sunny a different kind of look. It not only looked dead, it looked baffled.

John Dale gripped the tail tightly with his fingertips and began to rake the spoon harshly across the side of the fish, stripping off scales. They flaked away easily, and in less than a minute he'd cleaned all the way down to the smooth silvery-yellow skin.

Next, he slipped the edge of the spoon under the bony fins jut-ting from the fish's sides and, with two quick motions toward the head, snapped the sharp bones off into the sink. To remove the dorsal fin, he made a cut with one of his grandmother's old par-ing knives across the ridge of the back, just below the base of the fin, and pulled it forward toward the head. It peeled away easily.

So far everything was going as smoothly as he could have hoped for, and he began to wish, in spite of himself, that Sheila were here to witness his success. She would never have believed him capable.

"You'd never make it in the wilderness," she had told him, laughing at the fuss he made when the hook caught in his thumb.

"I could do all right," he said, trying to suppress his indignation. He swished his fingers through the water to wash away the blood.

"I'm sure every man likes to think that. But not many could." She began to wave her pole back and forth, drawing her float in a meandering zigzag across the shallows.

"There's no bait on that," he said, pointing out toward the line.

"I know. I'm trying it the hard way." She fished in silence while he rummaged through the tackle box for a Band-Aid. "What would you do if there was a war?" she asked suddenly.

"What do you mean?" He gave up on the Band-Aid and picked up the pole again.

"If there was a war—a nuclear war—and our whole society collapsed, what would you do to survive?"

"I don't think it'll ever come to that."

She slapped the frail tip of her pole against the surface of the lake.

"Which means if it ever does come to that, you won't know what to do." She touched the tip of her pole to the water again, this time so gently it barely made a ripple. Then she said something else, but she spoke so softly that John Dale couldn't quite catch it all. Something about marriage. He didn't ask her to repeat it.

He pulled up his line to check his bait. Small fish had been picking at his hook, and he had only half a worm left. While he loaded up the hook with part of another worm, he thought about what he would do to survive if society ever did collapse.

"I'd go to the library," he said finally. She turned to him and frowned. "I'd take out books on carpentry, and mechanics, farming, and whatever else looked like it might help me get along. With a knapsack full of the right books, I think I could survive anywhere, indefinitely." He was pleased with his reasoning, but Sheila remained unimpressed. She tossed a pebble into the water by his float.

"And while you're checking out library books, everybody else will be getting guns. You wouldn't stand a chance." She shook her head but smiled, as if he were a lost cause she couldn't quite abandon. "Survival isn't something you can look up in the reference section."

The sunny was ready now, either for gutting or having its head removed. He couldn't remember which was supposed to come first, or even if it mattered. He opted for decapitation, and sawed efficiently through the fish just behind the gills. After that it was easy to slit the underside and scrape out the organs into the sink.

He held the fish open before him like a book and thought about the bones. They seemed thoroughly enmeshed in the soft white meat, and he wasn't sure how to go about stripping them away without tearing up the remainder of the fish. He tried pulling at the spine, but that didn't work at all: the fish seemed to disintegrate in his hands. By the time he'd picked away all the tiny ribs, only two bite-sized pieces remained. Not much to show for his efforts. But if he could salvage at least this much meat from each of these dozen fish, that would be enough for a meal for the two of them. Sheila wouldn't eat much anyway. She was probably filling up now on steak and quail.

The catfish began to crawl around over the other fish. John Dale hated to see this. All he wanted was for them to die peacefully in their oxygen-starved comas. He didn't want to have to force matters.

Damned catfish. John Dale remembered a news story he'd seen about walking catfish. Someplace down in Florida people kept finding catfish in their yards. The fish were just passing through, looking for more hospitable waters. Their old haunts had been polluted by a chemical spill, so they had taken to the land, dragging themselves hundreds of yards, using their front fins like little crutches.

This catfish might take a very long time to die.

When he had fished these parts as a boy, his grandmother had never let him keep a catfish. "Too much trouble to clean," she always said. Catfish didn't have scales; they had to be skinned.

"I'll skin it," he always volunteered.

"I'd have to show you how, and I just don't want to mess with it. Anytime you hook a catfish, just throw him right back in."

That was always the rule. No turtles, no bream smaller than your hand, and no catfish whatsoever. As far as John Dale knew, this was the only catfish that had ever made it to her kitchen sink.

He set the catfish aside and continued working on the other fish. When he came to the first large-mouthed bass, he thought again of Sheila. This was the first fish she had caught, and after she'd swung it from the water to the lake bank, she'd insisted that he be the one to remove it from her line. He grumbled, but set about doing it. Then just as he finally dislodged the hook from the fish's throat, she swatted at a bee with her pole. He saw it coming, even had his mouth open to tell her not to move, but it was too late. The hook was deep in his thumb before he could utter a sound.

He looked again at his damaged thumb. It was turning a bluish white around the snag. He turned the tap on full again, thinking he should try to clean the wound before working on any more fish, and stuck his thumb under the stream. He wondered when he last had a tetanus shot, or even if a tetanus shot would help. He thought about particles of worm in his blood.

He didn't mind the pain of the water slicing into his cut. Pain that came with a cleansing was a good pain, he believed. Besides, he was convinced that treating injuries gently only heightened the agony.

The wound looked pretty clean, but the stink was still there. He squeezed some dishwashing liquid onto his fingers to cover up the odor. After he rinsed this off, his hands smelled even worse—still fishy-wormy, but now slightly sweet.

The catfish moved again, revived by the running water. John Dale quickly shut off the tap. The last thing he wanted was to keep this fish alive. He had to admit, though, it was quite a cat-fish. Even the dove hunters had admired it.

They'd heard his yelling when Sheila jerked the hook through his thumb, and came down from the woods to see what the trouble was. Sheila had been uneasy when she first saw the group approaching.

"Relax," he told her. John Dale knew there was nothing to worry about: the social structure hadn't fallen yet. Besides, this lake belonged to one of his father's cousins, so the chances were pretty good that somebody in the bunch would turn out to be a relative. He was right.

"Sheila, this is my cousin Boyd," he said, gesturing toward a bulging, round-faced, amiable-looking man. The man shifted his shotgun to the crook of his left arm and extended his hand.

"I'm Lewis," he said. "Boyd's my brother. Glad to meet you, Sheila." John Dale felt like a fool.

"Sorry, Lewis," he apologized. "Guess I must need glasses."

"Wish I'd known you were in town, you could've gone dove hunting with us."

"We just got in last night." John Dale nodded toward a bulging sack dangling from the shoulder of one of the other men. "But it looks like you did all right without me."

"Well," said Lewis, "first day of the season is always good." He pointed to the pile of fish. "Seems you've had some luck yourself. That catfish is a beauty."

"We've got plenty, if you'd like to take some along," John Dale offered.

Lewis smiled. "No, thanks, we've got steaks waiting for us up at the cabin. How about you two joining us? We've sure got more birds than we'll know what to do with. And you can't beat a steak and dove combination. Might even scrounge up some quail."

"That's real nice of you, Lewis, but I guess we'll just stick with our fish."

Lewis shrugged. "Well, suit yourself."

John Dale felt the need to explain further, but there was nothing to say.

After Lewis and his buddies had climbed back up the slope through the trees, John Dale put aside his pole and emptied the bait carton onto the bank. A few startled worms tumbled into the water.

"Giving up?" Sheila asked, nudging the overturned carton with her toe.

"I guess we've caught enough."

"Suits me." She dropped her own pole onto the grass beside John Dale. "Maybe you'd like to reconsider joining your cousin for dinner." John Dale pretended not to hear. He carefully wound her line around the top section of bamboo and tucked the barb of the hook into the clip of the plastic float. She asked him again.

"You go ahead if you want to," he said, winding his own line tightly around his pole.

"I really don't want to eat these fish," she said. They were quiet for a long time after that, and John Dale wondered if that meant they'd reached a decision.

"What about you?" he asked, breaking the silence. "What would you do if there was a nuclear war?"

She stared out across the lake. "Whatever I had to, I suppose."

"But I mean, would you stay with me?"

Sheila smiled and brushed her hair back from her face. "Only if you change your game plan."

He thought about that as he put the fish and the tackle into the back of the car. Change his game plan. Just what did she want? He was still thinking about it when he got into the car and drove away.

And now he thought about it again as he stood poised over the sink, knife in hand, waiting for the catfish to die. It was so hard to know what people really wanted. Maybe he'd been too hasty, maybe he shouldn't have left her there. Maybe he'd gone about everything wrong.

The catfish crawled against the side of the sink, looking for some way out. For a long time John Dale watched it scratching at the porcelain, watched the gray gills pulsing in and out. At last he took a washtub from beneath the sink and filled it, then picked up the big fish in both hands and slid it gently down into the fresh water.

He carried the washtub very carefully to the car, not spilling a drop.

THE LAST WARM DAY IN ALABAMA

One thing I struggle with is fear. Nothing original in that, I realize. We all own plots in that cemetery. But my case might be a little different from most in that I can trace the bulk of my nightmares back to a particular moment in my life, a single instant on a summer morning at the freight yards, where I'd gone to steal coal from abandoned railroad cars.

I was eleven years old, and on that day my friend Tippy Weaver and I had hiked down to the Cahaba River like we did most every summer morning. The county had gotten its share of rain that spring, and even the summer had been damp, but a June drought to the north of us had left the water level low enough that we could wade long stretches with just our pant legs rolled. We each carried a Mason jar for minnows, which were plentiful in the shady spots along the western bank, and which we could sell for a quarter to Andy's Bait Shop just across the trestle.

We also each carried a sharpened bamboo spear, about five feet long, which we had whittled from broken fishing poles. Our intention was to use these spears to fend off any copperhead or water moccasin we might inadvertently provoke. Tippy claimed to have seen four snakes already that summer, but one of those turned out to be a broken fan belt, so in truth he might not have seen any at all. I sure never did. But we were Alabama boys, after all, and welcomed any excuse to carry a weapon.

We worked our way up to the third bend, crossing out of Cahaba Heights and into Irondale. From there we cut through the marshy flood plain to Shades Creek and, crossing over, climbed the sandstone bank behind Blackie's Gentlemen's Club, a low, cinder block dive on Front Street across from the Norris freight yards.

Blackie's was a mystery of the adult world to us then, with neon cocktail glasses on the sign above the door, and windows haphazardly blackened with slapped-on coats of paint. On the far side, across the gravelly pockmarked street, was a string of coal cars that had sat untended for more than a year, each slowly filling with season after season of rain. They'd long ago been emptied of their loads, though not entirely. Most still held scatterings of coal beneath the stagnant water in the bottoms of the cars.

Wading those coal cars was easier than wading the Cahaba, or even Shades Creek, because the footing was firm and we had no worry about snakes. The bottoms were't even slimy, although I can't explain why. Maybe the compartments were treated with chemicals. Maybe the coal dust somehow kept the water too gritty and poisoned even for scum. Maybe it was just too damn hot. In any case the texture along the iron beds stayed rough enough for our bare feet to find traction. We still had to move with care, because the open cars were a favorite target for drunks with empty bottles. So we slid our feet carefully through the black water, nudging aside the shards of broken glass as we scavenged for the coal. Tippy kept a burlap bag tied to the belt loops of his jeans, and in less than half an hour we could pluck out enough burnable chunks to fill it.

This piecemeal dredging of the coal cars was not a pleasant activity, especially on a sweltering summer day, when those rust-coated sides burned hot enough to raise a blister. But we weren't doing it for fun. Tippy's family was pretty bad off, even by local standards. His dad was an older guy, over sixty, who'd lost his job at the Shell station because they thought he'd been stealing empty oil drums. Free coal was a real windfall for the Weavers because it meant they could heat their house come winter. That might not seem like a big deal, this being mid-Alabama where it almost never snows. But the Weavers' house was mostly tar paper, so it didn't have much in the way of insulation, and January, even around here, can get cold. If the temperature drops to thirty-five overnight, that's what you get out of bed to in the morning. Besides that, the Weavers had one of those old potbellied cookstoves—the only one I've seen in real life—and Mrs. Weaver fixed all their meals on it. So the coal made a difference there, too.

In six weeks we'd lugged home nearly three hundred pounds. A couple of times Mr. Weaver gave me a nickel for my part, but usually he paid me in magazine pages. He'd tear out big color pictures of pretty women in lipstick ads and give them to me. That seems kind of creepy to me now, but at the time I thought it was a pretty good salary. So just about every day we'd bring in a full sack, which we'd then carry around back of the chicken coop and empty into one of Mr. Weaver's oil drums.

To this day, coal still seems like some kind of miracle fuel to me. It never rots, it never gets eaten by termites, it won't go bad like gasoline. It's a rock that burns. And on top of all that, it's where diamonds come from.

Anyway, Tippy and I were just starting our first slow sweep through the murky water of an old Southern Railway car. Most of the coal cars were black, but this one was a dingy rust-red, older, I think, than the others. It was directly across Front Street from Blackie's, close enough that I could have hit the front screen door with the right piece of coal. On other days, in fact, I had done just that. Kids throw things, that's a simple fact, and even though it had cost us some effort to collect the coal, after climbing back out of the cars, sunbaked and soggy, and filthy beyond reason from the brackish water and our own stinking sweat, we couldn't resist flinging the occasional chunk toward the tubing of Blackie's neon cocktail sign. It was a natural target for an eleven-year-old—colorful, exotic, and highly breakable.

To my secret relief, we never hit it. We rarely even came close. Coal is pretty lightweight with a lot of facets and sheared edges. That meant the harder we threw, the more crazily each piece would carve its own path through the air. No big league pitcher ever had the kind of curve or slider we achieved involuntarily on every throw. Consequently, the entire cinder-block front, which had no windows, was peppered with our impact marks. Blackie must not have cared since, beyond putting dents in his screen door, we never really broke anything. In any case, he never washed the black marks away.

But on this day, August 26, 1963, our last day ever to scavenge coal at the freight yards, Tippy and I never got the chance to try our luck against the sign. A car with a bad muffler pulled into the gravel lot next to Blackie's. We noticed because there was seldom any traffic along this stretch of Front Street, at least not during the day. The club didn't open until sometime in the evening, and there were no other businesses along that desolate stretch, no destination but the barricaded dead end overlooking the creek at the far end of the yards. From the belly of the coal car we heard the slow, noisy approach, then the faint pop of gravel, then silence as the motor died, then the slam of the car door.

Neither Tippy nor I had ever seen Blackie. He was a late-night phantom known by reputation only. His Gentlemen's Club, a brown-bag private drinking establishment in an otherwise dry township, was famous throughout the valley as the embodiment of danger to both body and soul. Our minister at Trinity Methodist, Dr. Kimbrough, had used the word *vice* in decrying the activities of the place, and even though our parents rarely spoke about the specific goings-on, rumors of knife fights and drunken brawls circulated regularly through the schoolyard. It was said he was a bootlegger, that family fortunes had been lost at his poker table, that he rented out women for a dollar. He was the richest and most notorious man in all the Shades Valley towns, and to those of us in bed by nine o'clock, he was a figure of underworld myth, rivaling Al Capone, or Legs Diamond, or Pretty Boy Floyd. Or even the Devil himself.

"Maybe it's him," Tippy whispered, and he quickly began to untie the burlap sack from his waist. While he fumbled with the wet knots, I pulled myself up the sloping wall to take a look. A brief glimpse was all I could manage, because the rim of the car was like a stove top, so I couldn't hold on. As I slid back down, Tippy cast the coal sack aside and scrambled up the wall himself, burning his own fingers as I had done. With a sharp cry he leapt back down to the bottom of the car and plunged his hands into the dark water. After a few moments he straightened slightly and pressed his palms against his thighs. "I couldn't tell anything," he said hoarsely.

That was hardly a surprise. Tippy had poor eyesight, so poor they always made him sit up front in school. Nearsighted, I guess he was. His parents couldn't pay for glasses, though, so he pretty much viewed the world through a perpetual squint. I often had to fill in the more distant details. My eyes were fine.

"Just some regular guy," I told him. I'd seen the man for barely an instant myself, and only from behind, as he disappeared beyond the screen door. He was thin and blond, I could tell that much, and he wore cutoff jeans and a T-shirt. I noticed he was sunburned along the backs of his arms and legs.

Tippy fished around for the coal sack, which had slipped beneath the water out of sight. "I have to go home," he said, lifting up the mouth of the sack and pulling the drawstrings tight.

I took the sack by the neck and raised it from the water with one hand. "It's not even half full," I said. "Your mama couldn't heat a chili pepper with a load this small."

Tippy sucked in a slow breath through gritted teeth, and I suddenly realized that the look on his face wasn't a squint but a grimace.

"I jumped on glass," he said.

"Lemme see."

He put a hand on my shoulder to steady himself and drew his foot from the water. Blood trickled from a thin slice along the soft skin of his instep. I held his foot and pressed carefully around the edges of the cut. A fresh trickle flowed from the end nearest his heel, and I wiped it away with my fingers.

"It's a little deeper right here," I said, pointing to the bloodier half of the gash. "But it doesn't look too bad. You feel any glass in there?"

"I don't think so," he said, squeezing his foot with his free hand. "It doesn't really hurt all that much."

"Well, let it bleed for a while," I told him, wiping my fingers on my shirt front. "That'll clean it out. And don't put it back in this water—no telling what kind of corruption we're standing in."

"Maybe I'll get lockjaw," he said.

"Maybe you will."

Tippy smiled at the possibility. It was always good to imagine a little drama in our lives. "I'll pour peroxide on it when I get home," he said.

"Peroxide's for little kids," I told him. "Put something on it that stings, like iodine, or tincture of merthiolate. That's how you kill germs."

"Alcohol," he declared. "I'll pour alcohol right down inside the wound."

"I bet you won't," I said.

"I will, too." Tippy took the coal sack and tossed it over the rim of the car toward Front Street. "I ain't afraid of alcohol."

He pressed his foot carefully against the rough slope of the wall and stretched forward, hooking his fingers over the edge. He hoisted himself quickly up the incline and swung down on the other side. I followed him up over the rim and dropped beside him in the yellow dust.

"You talking about wood alcohol or grain?" I asked.

"Grain, you dope. Wood alcohol makes you go blind."

"Only if you drink it, moron. Anyway, where you gonna find grain alcohol? Your daddy don't allow it in the house. I heard him say so."

"There's other people got it," he said, but without much conviction.

"Name one," I challenged him.

Tippy looked down at the ground and shrugged. His parents belonged to the Temperance Union and were Holy Rollers besides. Liquor simply didn't exist in their world, except as the principal villain in countless cautionary tales. Tippy had a better chance of finding a penguin in his mother's pantry than a jug of moonshine or a bottle of Jack Daniel's.

I picked up the coal sack and tested the heft again—five or six pounds, at the most. I handed it to Tippy, and while he retied the sack to his belt loops I turned my attention to the minnow jars. The minnows were still moving, but instead of darting back and forth, they now cruised slowly around the curve of the jar. We needed to change the water soon or we'd lose them.

That was one lesson we'd learned the hard way. Most days we'd be lucky to snag half a dozen or so, because minnows were quick and difficult to catch bare-handed. But one day we hit the jackpot—stumbled into a whole school bunched up in a narrow stretch where Fuller Creek met the river. We could have reached in with our eyes closed and still brought out a handful. I'd never seen anything like it. Of course our greed got the best of us and we kept putting more and more minnows in the jars until finally they were packed in so tight they could barely wiggle. By the time we got them to the bait shop, they were all dead. Not enough oxygen in the water.

Today, too, we'd had good luck, finding a clotted run of minnows in a shallow pocket along the riverbank. This time we showed a little more restraint, but it was tough to resist overloading the jars when the minnows were right there for the taking. Maybe we'd been too greedy once again, though I couldn't tell yet. There's always a line between enough and too much, but it's hard to know where that line is until you've crossed it.

Tippy picked up one of the jars and, using his bamboo spear for balance, limped a few steps to the shoulder of the road. He stopped there, as if he were waiting for a break in traffic, and I noticed the small drips of blood that trailed behind him on the hard-packed ground.

"What's the matter?" I asked, coming up alongside him. "Mama won't let you cross the street by yourself?"

Tippy nodded toward the building in front of us. "I'll tell you somebody who's got grain alcohol," he said.

I laughed. "Blackie's got it, all right. And I guarantee he'll be keeping it, too. Here, gimme that." I took his minnow jar from him and handed him my stick of bamboo. "You'll shake 'em up too much, the way you're walking."

"You don't know what Blackie might do," Tippy said. "He might give us a little bit, if we asked for it. Just for medicine."

"Yeah, right." I held the two jars still for a minute to let the cloudiness settle, and then started across the street. At the edge of Blackie's gravel lot I turned back toward Tippy, who stood rooted to his spot.

"I bet he's got Band-Aids, too." He lifted his foot and rapped the shorter bamboo spear against his heel to shake loose some of the freight-yard grit. "Probably be glad to help us out." A smug smile crept across his face. "Unless you're scared to ask."

"Just get your butt across the street," I said.

At that moment, I don't know if I meant to take his dare or not. Tippy wasn't hurt that bad, but a sliced-open foot could be a legitimate excuse to knock on Blackie's door. I knew there was no chance to get any alcohol from him. No man in the Church-led county was crazy enough to give liquor to kids in those days. He'd get himself run out of town, or maybe worse. Alabama was well known as an inhospitable place for a lot of people back then. But if we somehow got to talk to Blackie himself, face to face, even if it was for just a second, we could be big shots in the neighborhood from then on.

Tippy eased his way across to me, using the bamboo shafts like crutches. "What about it, Tay? Got enough guts?"

"These minnows are winding down fast," I told him.

"They ain't no worse off than I am," he said. "I'm the one still bleedin'." He spat into the gravel to show his disgust. "You're just chicken, is all."

I looked over at Blackie's dented screen door, not ten steps away, and shook my head. "Least I'm not stupid."

That was the wrong thing for me to say. Stupidity was a sore spot with Tippy because he was, in fact, stupid. He was the only kid anyone knew who had actually failed the first grade, and this year he had failed the fourth. He didn't say anything at first, but I could see from the way he tightened his jaw and stared past me down the street that I'd made him mad. I knew he was calculating his next move, but I couldn't guess what it might be. We often pretended to be cruel or tough with each other, and sometimes, without our meaning for it to happen, we'd go too far, and that familiar moment of crisis would suddenly arrive. I recognized that moment now as Tippy took a long slow breath and raised up the longer of the two bamboo spears—the one that was mine.

"I'll show you stupid," he said, and before I could make a move to stop him, he let it fly, full force, toward the doorway. It was a perfect throw, one that tore through the center of the rusty mesh and lodged there, half in and half out of Blackie's old screen door. We both froze, then, neither one of us believing the line that Tippy had just dared to cross.

I don't know why we didn't run. My whole life would have turned out differently if we had. But recklessness is its own kind of liquor and can swamp the mind in a hurry. Without a word passing between us, Tippy and I began to move toward the damaged door, daring each other forward with every tentative step.

When we reached the pitted concrete slab that footed the doorway, I tucked the jar from my right hand—Tippy's jar—into the crook of my left elbow and reached out to retrieve the spear. It was right then, before I'd even begun to pull the bamboo from the screen, that we heard the first muted shot. We both jumped, and Tippy's jar tumbled forward onto the stoop, shattering in a splash of dying minnows and glass. Two more shots followed the first, and Tippy broke into a run, bad foot and all, and disappeared around the corner of the building before I could even sort things out clearly enough to react. For the longest four seconds of my life I stood stranded in confusion. I needed to pick up the broken glass. I needed to scoop up the minnows, I needed to take back my spear, I needed to run. But I couldn't think or even move. I couldn't do anything but stand there in the exact wrong place at the exact wrong time, as muffled shouts and curses rolled forward from some back room in Blackie's club.

Then the sound of an inner door banging open.

Of chairs flung against a wall.

Of a table overturning.

Of the bursting clatter of things going to pieces, scattering in all directions across the floor.

Then three more shots, much louder this time, much nearer the front, and the rising up of shadows beyond the screen, and the gasping cry of the large man now barreling toward me from the shallow darkness of the club.

I thought I was killed for certain. But still I couldn't move, even as the screen door banged open and Blackie, it had to be Blackie, lunged across the threshold, stumbling through the broken glass and pitching forward, his heavy body colliding with mine in a glancing blow that sent me flying to one side as he skidded awkwardly to his knees in the gravel.

He knelt there, head down, blood drooling in strands from his gaping mouth, struggling to breathe. I don't think he even realized I was there, or if he did, he was far beyond caring. He coughed a couple of times and vomited weakly into his hands, then settled slowly back on his heels. I remember expecting him to fall over, but he didn't, he stayed slumped on his knees, his head resting on his chest, like a man in prayer. Like a statue, that's how still he was. Then it occurred to me that he was dead.

I looked toward the doorway, hoping to God the thin blond man would not be there yet, that I would still have time to run, like Tippy did, and leave this nightmare behind me. But what I saw there scoured every small hope from my heart. The screen had not swung shut—the shaft of bamboo had been knocked nearly free when Blackie forced the frame back against the outer cinderblock wall, and now the sharpened end of the spear drooped into the dirt beside the stoop, propping the door wide open. There in the entryway, with the gun still in his hand, was the thin blond man I'd seen before, only this time I recognized him. It was Billy Hatcher, who lived on my block just two houses down. Billy had spent time in reform school, but everybody around knew there was nothing reformed about him.

He stepped out onto the stoop and glanced around. I looked around, too, hoping for some policeman on patrol, some passing car, some hobo headed for the river, anything that might somehow alter my situation. But the street was deserted—no people, no stray dogs, no birds, no presence of any kind. No sound but the soft grumbling of a distant train, no movement but the small halo of dust stirred up by Blackie when he fell. Billy calmly raised his pistol, aimed it at my face, and pulled the trigger. The empty click surprised him.

"Fuck," he yelled, and started toward me. I tried to scramble away, but he was too quick and too close, and before I could get halfway to my feet he caught me by the back of my shirt and dragged me toward the open doorway.

But I wasn't feeling so paralyzed anymore. The monster here wasn't the terrifying phantom of my imagination that Blackie had been. The monster here was my asshole neighbor Billy, a skinny punk with no more bullets in his gun, a flesh-and-blood human being with a flesh-and-blood susceptibility to pain.

As he hoisted me up over the edge of the stoop into the minnows and broken glass, I reached down with my free hand and jerked loose the piece of bamboo from the open screen door. He must have seen me make the grab, because he stopped mid-stride and slammed me on my stomach against the concrete slab, smashing the second jar of minnows beneath me. I knew I was cut, but it didn't matter, and even with the wind knocked out of me, I could still maneuver. I squirmed sideways in his grip and rammed the spear upwards as hard as I could, up the left pant leg of his baggy cutoffs, catching him on the inside of his upper thigh. Bamboo, if you carve it right, allows a sharper edge than ordinary wood—stronger, too, and more blade-like—and now I was able to push the narrow point deep into a knot of muscle. His whole body tightened involuntarily, and in that split second of delay, before he could react in my direction, I twisted the shaft and shoved it further in. Billy howled and staggered sideways, dropping me before I could stab him again. He rolled onto his back in the gravel and grabbed his bleeding leg with both hands.

"Goddammit!" he screamed, and the rage in his voice was so fierce I thought he might come after me again that very instant, in spite of any damage I had done. But the wound, apparently, was a good one, and for the moment Billy stayed where he was—as did I, because the wind was still knocked out of me, and I couldn't yet run. So for an oddly calm handful of seconds we both just lay there, hurting, in the gravel, with the dead man propped absurdly between us, fighting our separate battles to regain control. Blackie's screen door, I remember, creaked on its hinges and slowly swung shut.

But soon enough my breath came back, and I was on my feet again. At first I thought to break toward the river, but Tippy had gone that way and might still be waiting for me just behind the building. Besides, the flood plain offered no place to hide and was too swampy for running, and if Billy caught me too near the river he could drown me. My best bet was higher ground.

I lit out across the road toward the freight yards, and even though I heard Billy slipping in the gravel behind me, I didn't look back, not then, because I didn't want to know how quick he still might be, or how close, or how crazy. I didn't want to know anything.

I just ran. I ran past the line of coal cars, and across three sets of empty track, and past the loading docks for the Birmingham Southern, and the Central of Georgia, and the Seaboard Line, and then I veered between equipment sheds and dodged a handcar overturned in the weeds, and raced along a drainage ditch, and jumped the ditch when it angled toward the river, and my lungs burned and my side ached, but I kept running because I had no choice, and I ducked beneath a row of cattle cars on the Great Alabama Southern, and sprinted past the holding pens and past a switching spur, and came out, finally, on the far north side of the rails, up by the main tracks, where at that blessed moment a string of boxcars rumbled slowly along the upper end of the yards.

My legs were nearly spent, but I set the lumbering boxcars as my goal and forced myself into a final kick, a last, desperate burst that carried me up alongside an empty car, up within reach of the iron ladder bolted to its wall. The ground was level and the train was slow, so it was a simple matter to grab a high rung and gain a foothold, and, from there, to work my way up the ladder and step through the open boxcar door.

That's when I finally looked back, down that long cluttered slope toward the flood plain and the river. But there was nothing to see; Billy was nowhere behind me. Maybe I'd lost him in the rail yards. Or maybe he hadn't chased me after all, maybe he was still on his back in the gravel. Or maybe he'd driven home to put more bullets in his gun. I didn't like not knowing, but that part was out of my hands because the boxcar came with a limited view, and Blackie's place was hidden now by too many other things, too many sheds, and warehouses, and train cars, and trees. Even the midmorning sun glared against me.

I stepped away from the opening into the shadows of the car and sank to the straw-littered floor. The mild vibration of the tracks hummed in my spine, and I began to shake uncontrollably. I wish I could blame that on shock or sheer exhaustion, but the truth of the matter is that a raw fear capsized me entirely, thumping through my rib cage and choking away my breath.

I can't say why. I mean, I'd already escaped. When a storm is over we come up from the cellar, we don't cower in a corner waiting for the next big blow. The train had carried me beyond Billy's physical reach, so by rights I should have been dancing, regardless of whatever new knowledge had come my way. Besides, I knew I could find safety with the next sheriff down the line—which, in fact, I did. Billy got arrested and was sent away. But there in that boxcar something big and dark had taken hold, as if the entire world had staked a new claim inside me.

I looked down at my T-shirt, mottled with blood, and brushed my shaking fingers lightly across the cotton to feel for glass. A few small splinters glistened in the weaving, and when my hand steadied enough, I picked the slivers out as carefully as I could. It calmed me to have something small and appropriate like that to focus on, something clear and uncomplicated. But some things can't be salvaged, and after a few minutes I peeled off the shirt and tossed it out the door into the weeds. Then I leaned back against the dark metal wall of the boxcar. The rough steel felt cool against my bare skin, and even though this was summertime in Alabama, a chill gradually crept through me.

To this day, I can feel it still.

BUT THEN FACE TO FACE

After consulting with Reverend Tyree, Patty Hatton felt less inclined to kill her husband, Bryce. She hadn't told the Reverend outright what she wanted to do, hiding her intentions behind a series of clever *What ifs*, but she still got the sense that he was discouraging her. Most of what he told her was aimed at shoring up her righteousness—platitudes she'd heard before about forgiveness and love and not killing people.

But that had been on Thursday, with Bryce in jail and the church still a church. A lot had happened since then. For one thing, there'd been the fire. The wrath of God had come down hard on First Baptist, rebuking it clear to its foundation. If Reverend Tyree had possessed any real understanding of God's ways, he should have seen that coming, he should have known that putting a toaster next to the curtains in the annex kitchen was practically daring God to do something. But no, he'd been blindsided right along with everyone else. So the Reverend was probably no more plugged in than Madam Zubu the Mysterious.

Then there was Bryce's ridiculous escape attempt that had put him in the hospital, which was a hopeful sign. People died in hospitals all the time.

She considered waiting to see if that might happen. If Walter could die from an allergic reaction to a painkiller on his way to the hospital, surely Bryce could die from a three-story leap. But in the end she lacked the patience for that kind of vigil.

Still, killing Bryce would be a big step, and she didn't want to make a mistake, so she opened up her New Testament, figuring if anybody could offer guidance, it would be Jesus. She was right.

A man's foes shall be they of his own household, Jesus told his disciples. *I came not to send peace, but a sword.*

Clearly, Jesus understood her situation. It was entirely possible that Jesus wanted Bryce dead, too.

She put their wedding photo into her handbag and set out for the hospital. She wasn't sure why she wanted the photo with her. There was nothing special about it—just the wedding party posed before the altar at First Baptist.

Then it occurred to her that everything in the picture was now gone from her life. Not just the sanctuary, but the people. Bryce, smiling and holding her hands. Walter, the best man, leering impishly over Bryce's shoulder. Ramona Wilkes, her maid of honor, whom she hadn't seen since that day, nearly nine months earlier, grinning stupidly by her side. Even the altar itself, where she and Bryce had consecrated their vows, had turned to ash.

The more she thought about it, the more she realized that her wedding photo had evolved into a summary of the worst failures of her life. She imagined pinning it to Bryce's chest with a steak knife.

As she walked up Green Street toward the hospital, she was surprised at how normal everything looked. The daffodils were coming into bloom. Lawns were cropped short, hedges were trimmed, trees stood leafy and unbroken. The day was unseasonably warm, and the air had a spring-like freshness that reminded her of Easter. On any other afternoon, she might have mistaken the Creation for an orderly place. *God's in His Heaven, all's right with the world,* wasn't that how the poem went? But that was illusion. God was asleep on the job, and the world had spun completely off its axis. Otherwise, couldn't God have saved Walter from that simple ride in the ambulance? Or better yet, couldn't He have kept Walter from being shot in the first place? When the poker game had turned ugly, Bryce had meant to shoot Tom Parsons, not his own cousin Walter. But intentions didn't matter to the law. Bryce still had to stand trial for Walter's death, even though the bullet had only nicked him in the leg.

As she pushed her way through the front door to the admitting desk, the sharp, sour smell of the place nearly stopped her cold. The hallways reeked of the same pungent odor that had cloaked her father those days when she had visited his stills up the mountain. She had learned to despise that alcoholic stink in all its forms, and even though she understood the smell here to be medicinal and antiseptic, that didn't keep the queasiness from churning through her stomach.

The memory of her father bothered her as much as the smell itself. She hadn't seen him in months, and didn't want to. His contribution to her life had ended on her wedding day, as far as she was concerned. He hadn't even shown up to walk her down the aisle, but had gone on a three-day bender instead.

Not that her mother was much better. When she drank, her mind narrowed to a brick alleyway, with no room to turn around. That had been the case when the Bible salesman had come nosing up onto their porch. Her mother had mistaken him for a revenuer because of his dark suit, and, in spite of Patty's pleas to the contrary, she had attacked him with a shovel.

The receptionist at the admitting desk looked haggard in the waning afternoon light. Patty assumed she must have had a long day of preparing paperwork and answering the fearful questions of relatives and well-wishers.

She wondered who her own well-wishers might be if she ever ended up here. Her relatives had all slunk back into the woods for now, and might not emerge again for generations. Her town friends had moved away or gone to college or joined the army. Reverend Tyree might stop by, but his reasons would be strictly professional, impersonal, a shepherd keeping track of a wayward sheep, and a visit from him would only depress her.

She took a handkerchief from her pocketbook and held it over her nose as she looked around the crowded lobby. All the chairs were occupied by tired-looking women, and the men, some in wrinkled suit coats and some in jeans and sweatshirts, as if they'd just come in from playing softball, slouched against the walls, chatting in whispers. Churches and hospitals, those were the two places people kept their voices low, loosening their grip on whatever secrets had brought them there in the first place. Patty stepped up to the admitting desk and stood there, waiting to be acknowledged, but the haggard woman was absorbed and didn't look up.

"Excuse me, ma'am," Patty said. "I'm looking for Bryce Hatton. I understand he's a patient here."

The woman raised her eyes and studied Patty carefully over the top of her glasses. Then she picked up a clipboard and scanned down a row of names. "Maternity ward," she said. "Two floors up. Go left when you get off the elevator."

"He's in the maternity ward?"

"We've had a burst pipe and had to shut down the power on the fourth floor," the woman told her. "We've had to juggle things around a little bit today. But things should be back on track by tomorrow."

"Thank you," Patty said, though the notion of Bryce on the maternity ward unnerved her. Was this some kind of sign from the universe? If so, what could it possibly mean? She headed toward the elevators.

"You'll have to check in with the deputy when you get there," the woman called after her, and Patty felt the blood rise to her face. All eyes, she knew, would be staring at her now.

After an excruciatingly long wait, the metal door slid open and she stepped in beside an old man in green scrubs with a utility cart stacked with folded linens, presumably coming up from the basement level. An orderly, she imagined, though he appeared too ancient to still be on the job. But maybe this was what he had coming to him, maybe this was God's punishment for crimes of his youth. Yes, she could see it in his withered frame, and in the scaly features of his face, and the rheumy distance in his eyes. He had probably been cruel and reckless, committing unspeakable acts of violence or depravity, surviving this long only through selfishness and luck. Maybe there was a woman somewhere who would rejoice to know the world had closed in so tightly around him, reserving only the task of cleaning up hospital messes while he waited out the end of his days.

People were a disappointment—she had to remember that. Pity was a wasteful indulgence. Old men were pathetic because they deserved to be, because they had all once been young and smug and full of snakelike charm.

"Have a nice day, miss," he said hoarsely as she stepped off at the third floor.

She looked cautiously around. The floor seemed quiet, nearly deserted except for three people perched on a long, upholstered bench at the far end of the hall. One of them was a sheriff's deputy. He sat with his hands clasped in his lap and his head tilted back against the wall. His mouth hung open, and she guessed him to be asleep. The two women sitting next to him both looked vaguely familiar. They stared at her in silence.

Across from the elevator was the viewing window to the nursery, so Patty strolled over to pretend an interest in the newborns. All the bassinets were empty. There was only one baby on display, a girl, judging from the tiny pink cap and blanket, and she was in some kind of glass box with a heat lamp beaming down on her.

Get used to it, kid, she thought.

Funny that Bryce would be the one to make it to the maternity ward and not her. Maybe if she had gotten pregnant, things would have gone differently between them.

She shuddered at the thought. Bryce didn't drink, but in other ways he was even more insufferable than her father, always staying out late to play pool or cards, skipping work whenever he felt like it, and, after he got fired, spending money on a bass boat when they hadn't even paid the electric bill. Bryce was infantile at best, a terrible role model, and any child of his would have been further cursed with freakishly good looks and a crippling capacity for snide self-satisfaction. The spawn of Bryce Hatton would have bullied other children on the playground, cheated on tests, chalked obscenities on the blackboard, stolen lunch money from the cloakroom, spat on the cafeteria floor, lied to the principal, and vandalized the boys' and girls' bathrooms.

Perhaps she should start with castration.

Patty turned toward the women, who were now whispering together, and the deputy, whose mouth was now closed, and strode down the hall. But before she'd covered half the distance, one of the women rose from the bench and hurried forward to greet her.

"Patty, it's wonderful to see you again," the woman said, wrapping her in a warm hug. Then she gripped Patty by both shoulders and looked her up and down. "Look at you, all grown up," she said. "I might not have recognized you if Rose hadn't told me who you were."

Rose. Good Lord in Heaven. The other woman on the bench was Rose Hatton, her mother-in-law, who now sat stiffly in place, clutching her handbag in her lap, staring vacantly ahead. She didn't expect Rose to be civil—after all, Patty was the devil who had led her boy astray and then betrayed him. She probably blamed Patty for all of Bryce's failings, including the ones he had before he met her.

Rose had always looked out of place, no matter where she was, but today she appeared particularly uprooted. Her makeup was caked on the way a child might have applied it, and she had dyed her hair an unnatural strawberry blonde that resembled cotton candy. Her black, magnolia-patterned dress hung on her like a flour sack, and she looked ready for a long, uncomfortable bus ride. She and Patty had always tended to avoid each other, except at official family gatherings, and even then they staked out opposite ends of the yard. Still, Patty should have recognized her.

But who was this other woman? She was far better dressed and made-up than Rose, of a different class altogether. Her fixed smile showed a mouthful of even white teeth, which put her well outside Rose's parents' social circle. Maybe Patty had met her at the courthouse. A lawyer's wife, perhaps.

"I'm here to see Bryce," Patty said, glancing past the woman to the deputy, whose eyes were still closed.

"My son does not want to see you," said Rose, and the deputy opened his eyes.

He got to his feet and adjusted his belt and holster. He was a large man, the kind who would have played football in high school, with a round flat face and a bristle-cut of blond hair. "We have to keep a pretty tight rein on visitation, ma'am," he said. "Family members only."

"I'm his wife," she said.

Rose snorted, but didn't say anything.

The deputy glanced uneasily at Rose. "That counts," he told her.

"Try not to wake up Ramona," said the other woman, lowering her voice to a stage whisper. "I know she'd love to see you, but right now she's exhausted."

Of course. The woman was Mrs. Wilkes. Patty had met her a couple of times in high school, back when Ramona and Patty had been co-editors of the school newspaper. Mrs. Wilkes had served them lemonade once while they worked on layout at the Wilkes's dining room table and had warned them not to drip glue on the glossy veneer. Then Patty had seen her again at the wedding.

"What's wrong with Ramona?" Patty asked.

"Poor judgment," she said, rolling her eyes, and Patty remembered why Ramona used to complain so much about her mother. "And that baby's just the least of it."

"What baby?"

Mrs. Wilkes gestured toward the nursery. "That little girl in the incubator," she said. "She doesn't have a name yet. My granddaughter."

Ramona was a full year younger than Patty. How could she have a baby already? And when had she come home from college? Patty felt the color rise in her neck. The world was excluding her, bit by bit, carrying on its business in secret, changing the landscape every time she looked away. Well, she was sick of it, sick of this string of pop quizzes she hadn't known to study for. She needed to regain control.

"I'll only be a minute," she said.

The deputy held the door for her, and Patty entered the hospital room alone. She was surprised he didn't search her for weapons or hacksaws. Wasn't that what wives did for their jailbird husbands—bring them tools to make good their escape? Not that the deputy would have found anything to confiscate. For all her anger and her plans to cause Bryce harm, she'd forgotten to pack any useful hardware. The most dangerous thing she carried was an emery board.

The room was bright with afternoon sun. Ramona lay sleeping in the first bed, and even unconscious she looked like a wrung-out washrag. Her face was pink and blotchy, and her eyes had sunken into dark hollows, making her look years older. Her hair was matted to her forehead in a slick tangle of knots.

So that was motherhood.

Bryce looked far worse, rigged into his bed near the window with straps and pulleys. He wore a cast on each leg and on his left arm, while his right wrist was handcuffed to the bedrail. But his face was what she couldn't help staring at. All the delicately chiseled features of his face had been semi-obliterated, and stitches now held shut the gashes that had opened on his chin and cheekbones from the impact of his fall. His skin was purple, for the most part, and swollen so that his eyes were no more than slits. His nose was spread extravagantly across his face, as if the cartilage had been flattened out with a ball-peen hammer. His jaw seemed to fit crookedly in his skull. If she'd met him on the street, she'd have been more likely to peg him as a circus freak than as her husband.

She felt elated. Bryce had given himself the pounding he deserved and in the process left himself disfigured. True, the swelling would go down and his coloring would return to normal, but he'd never look like his old self again. From here on out, Bryce Hatton would be scarred. Unattractive. Maybe even ugly. The boy who thought he could coast through life on nothing but his good looks would have to change his plans.

She leaned over his face and peered into the purple slits, hoping for some flicker of recognition.

"I could do anything to you right now that I wanted," she hissed.

"He's not much fun," said Ramona.

Patty straightened and eased away toward the foot of the bed. Ramona stared at her with half-closed eyes and a feeble smile on her lips.

"They've got him all doped up," she added.

Patty put her hand on Bryce's leg cast and shook it, but he didn't respond. Then she shoved the cast hard, clacking it against the other leg. Bryce still lay undisturbed, breathing peacefully.

"You don't seem glad to see him," Ramona slurred.

"Go back to sleep," Patty told her. "You've got a baby to rest up for."

"I don't remember," she said. "They gave me some kind of super painkiller for the bad parts, and something else later on." She laughed softly. "I feel pretty good now."

"I can tell," said Patty. "Now go back to sleep."

"Did you see the baby?"

Patty sighed. "Yes."

"What's her name?"

Ramona hadn't been drinking, but she might as well have been, and Patty felt her annoyance building. She had long ago tired of coping with drunks, or crazies, or anyone else who couldn't keep a clear head. People were bad enough without shuffling wild cards into the deck.

"You haven't given her a name," Patty told her.

"Good," Ramona said. "Names limit a person."

Patty couldn't argue with that. *Mrs. Bryce Hatton* had been the sorriest limitation she'd ever known.

"The Tao that can be named is not the eternal Tao," Ramona declared. She stretched her arms over her head and yawned. "That's Chinese."

This was not the scene Patty had envisioned. Bryce was supposed to be awake, begging for his life. Ramona was supposed to be away at college—or anywhere else in the world, for that matter. Anywhere but here.

Ramona sat up in bed and pulled at a tangle in her hair. "You don't like me anymore," she said.

"No, Ramona, I don't."

"We were friends in typing class," she said. "I was in your wedding."

"You were also at the rehearsal."

Ramona narrowed her eyes and nodded. "I shouldn't have let Bryce kiss me," she said. "I know it looked bad. I was just trying to be polite."

That had been the moment, there in the alcove by the baptismal font, with Ramona backed into the corner and Bryce hunched over her, his hand edging up the side of the ugly bridesmaid's dress like he was about to cop a feel—that was when Patty had known she should call it off, that she should go tell Reverend Tyree that she'd changed her mind. She could have used her father as an excuse, told them all she couldn't get married without the old man there to give her away. But Bryce had snaked his way out of it, telling her she had it all wrong, that he was just celebrating with their friends. And maybe that's all it had been, maybe she had exaggerated everything in her mind because, deep down, she was afraid of what she was doing, afraid she didn't know how to be a wife. But still, the sight of Bryce pressing himself against another woman, even if the woman was just mousy little Ramona, had tripped an alarm in her brain, and she realized that this was a boy she would never fully trust, not if they lived to be a hundred.

She had wrestled with her doubts right up to the ceremony; beyond the ceremony, in fact, because the instant Reverend Tyree had pronounced them man and wife, her first thought was to beg for a do-over, another shot at getting the answers right. *Do you take this man?* the Reverend would ask again, and this time she would say, *No, no I don't—I suspect he's a no-good son of a bitch.* But it was too late. In the blink of an eye, organ music was sweeping them down the aisle, everyone was smiling and throwing rice, and her married life was already underway.

"Your ceremony was so beautiful," Ramona said. "That's when Hank and I decided to get serious."

"Good for you."

"He drove me home afterwards and I let him take off my bra. Things went pretty fast after that. I got pregnant the next weekend." She focused her eyes on Patty and nodded like she knew something important. "There's a lot of room in the back seat of a Chrysler."

So that was the story. Hank Motlow and Ramona Wilkes, high school sweethearts with a baby. They didn't stand a chance.

"Would you be my maid of honor?" asked Ramona. "If Hank's not dead, I mean."

He might indeed be dead, Patty realized. Vietnam was taking a heavy toll, and at this point they all knew boys who had died there. Jim Frazee, Dave Pickering, John Rice, the Hoylman kid who had sat behind her in homeroom. Curt Musselman from the farm next to her parents' place. Hank Motlow could easily join the list.

Bryce had been one of the few who had stayed behind, having blown out an eardrum playing with firecrackers when he was ten. Maybe that's why she had fallen for him—there wasn't anybody else around. The Selective Service had taken all the good ones. Nothing left but 4-F's and old-timers.

"Hank won't die," Patty said. But she knew the realities. Even if Hank Motlow made it home from Vietnam, and even if he felt guilty enough to marry Ramona when he got here, there would be no happily-ever-after for their situation. Patty had learned a lot typing transcripts at the courthouse, had read the trial testimony of countless couples who'd started out in love but ended up at each other's throats. She knew first-hand the way good intentions turned to dust. At best, Ramona and Hank would pack up their belongings and move to another town. Then they could live out their downfall among strangers, which would at least be less humiliating than failing at home.

"Bryce won't die either," Ramona offered. She meant it as a kindness, Patty knew, but still a thick curtain came down over her heart.

"I wish he would," she said.

Ramona bit her lip and frowned, and Patty could see she was struggling to concentrate.

"Why?" she asked.

No point hiding anything at this late date, she figured. Besides, by the time Ramona came out of her cloud, she'd have forgotten Patty was ever here.

"I loved somebody else," Patty said. "Bryce killed him."

Ramona opened her mouth, but no sound came out. She shook her head and lay back against her pillow. "I'm confused," she said at last.

"Walter Hatton," she explained.

"But you're married to Bryce," Ramona said.

"Bryce doesn't know what married is," said Patty, glancing toward him on the bed. "If he ever expected things to work out between us, he needed to stay home a few nights, not roam around like some stray dog."

"Not roam around," Ramona repeated. "That's right. It's bad to roam."

Patty realized she had trapped herself. If infidelity was the measure, she was every bit as guilty as Bryce. All he had on her was a head start.

"Can't be helped though," Ramona went on. "All roads lead to roam." She pulled the covers over her face and broke into muffled laughter.

Patty's first impulse was to slap her silly, but there was something ridiculously true in what she had said. Patty didn't know any couples her own age who had managed to stay faithful. None at all. Maybe Patty was as immature as Bryce, and Ramona, and Hank, and all the rest. Maybe they were all just too young, too volatile, too full of expectations to settle into the kind of commitment marriage was meant to be.

Maybe she would have failed with Walter just as she had failed with Bryce.

"That may be the smartest thing you ever said," Patty told her.

Ramona stopped her giggling and sat up again, allowing the bedsheet to fall from her face. "I might have heard it from a dead man," she announced, and collapsed dramatically onto her back again.

That was another thing Patty hated about drugs and alcohol. They gave people false visions, imaginary visits from all manner of ghosts and hobgoblins. Her father once thought their living room rug was a sea of live rats trying to devour his legs.

But this one wasn't Ramona's fault. The doctors had pumped her full of their own special brand of delirium, and she had no choice but to ride it out.

She looked again at Bryce. She didn't feel like killing him anymore. The core of her malice had simply drained away. Bryce was just a haughty child—Patty, too, for that matter, and their mistakes would haunt them both for years. All she wanted now was for Bryce to live long enough to regret who he was, long enough to feel shame at how thoughtlessly he had destroyed the dreams of those around him.

"I'll be your maid of honor, Ramona," she said, but the girl had already drifted back to sleep. Patty opened her pocketbook and took out the wedding photo. Ramona looked good in the picture, probably better than she would ever look again, given what lay ahead. Patty propped it on the table by her bed. Times had changed. It should be Ramona's keepsake now.

She reached back into her pocketbook and fished out the Shafer fountain pen she used at the courthouse for signing legal documents. She would be the first to sign Bryce's cast. All three casts, in fact. When he finally woke, that would be the first thing he saw: her name written over and over on the plaster of his arm and of both legs, filling the white space with evidence of who she was.

Not Mrs. Bryce Hatton. Never again Mrs. Bryce Hatton. She would use her maiden name, and he would have no choice but to read *Patricia Elaine Hart* all day long, whenever he opened his eyes. *Patricia Elaine Hart,* until all his bones had healed.

Yes, from here on out it would be *Patricia Elaine Hart.*

That name, too, was limiting. But at least it left her room to move around.

MUSIC FOR HARD TIMES

Jimmy swept the last bits of loose turf into his dustpan and slowly scanned the pro shop floor: it still looked filthy. Two hundred golfers had tracked the mud in all day long, and now their grimy trafficways branched from the doorway like shadows, darkening each aisle. Sweeping couldn't clean that kind of dirt; he'd have to wash the whole floor with a scrub brush and ammonia.

He didn't mind, though. The extra work gave him an extra excuse to stay late, and staying late gave him the opportunity to go through the members' golf bags for loose change. On a good Sunday night he could fish out thirty or forty bucks, no sweat, which gave him just the boost he needed to cover his food bills and his rent. It was a great fringe benefit to a job he already thought was perfect.

Absolutely perfect. Why else would he have passed up college to stay here? When Dickinson offered him the golf scholarship, he had almost taken it. But then he realized that a chance to play college golf wasn't reason enough to leave. He could play all the golf he wanted right here. Rod had made him the assistant pro, and that meant free greens fees for as long as he kept his job. He took advantage of it, too, spending more time on the course than the richest members of the Club. Scrubbing an occasional late-night floor was a small price to pay for all that.

And so what if it had pissed his father off?

He found the steel bucket under the sink in the mop closet and had just filled it with hot water when he heard a sharp tapping on one of the windows out front. "We're closed," he shouted, and poured some cleaner into the bucket. The tapping came again, louder this time and more insistent, but he ignored it. He'd worked here long enough to know what to expect on the last night of a tournament: drunks on the prowl. One or two always managed to drift down from the closing dinner-dance when the polka band broke after its first set. They'd think because the light was on they could come in and browse, maybe pick up a cheap new sweater for the wife. But Rod never left him the key to the cash drawer, so there wasn't much he could do but shoo people away. Sometimes, though, they were hard to get rid of, especially once he'd let them in the shop. He tried his best not to despise them.

The older guys were harmless enough—they just got talkative when they got tanked up and always battered him with lame advice: he should stick with school and get a good education, he should make the most of his youth, he should get regular dental checkups. Sometimes they'd crack some feeble joke, or quiz him on the details of his life. It all followed a pretty standard drill—the avuncular middle-American posturing he'd expect from any grade school principal, Bible salesman, or TV weatherman.

The younger drunks were a different story. The guys in their late twenties or early thirties seemed to want to prove they were still nineteen, like Jimmy, and if he let them get a foot in the door, it was all he could do to keep them from trashing the place. Most of them acted pissed off about their lives—their jobs weren't making them rich, their golf scores weren't low enough, their drug connections weren't reliable, and their wives were starting to catch on to what wretches they were. The young drunks were the ones who worried him because he knew where they were headed.

He dropped a scrub brush into the ammonia water and lifted the bucket from the sink, sloshing a warm wave over the rim onto his sneakers. He stood for a moment in the doorway listening: muted fragments of an accordion tune strayed unevenly through the bank of closed windows, the faint notes mingling with highway noise and distant bursts of clubhouse laughter. The tapping had stopped, but now he could hear voices rising in conversation on the pro shop porch, and Jimmy knew he was stuck. Single drunks tended to wander away if he ignored them, but when they came in pairs they were more tenacious, clinging doggedly to their own fuzzy game plans regardless of what he said or did.

He carried the bucket to the front of the shop and set it on the rubber mat by the door. As he reached into the gray water for the scrub brush, one of the people on the porch began to rattle the storm door.

"Jimmy! Open up!"

He recognized Teddy Mumford's voice. Teddy was one of the high-profile members, partly because he was the club's insurance agent and, at twenty-eight, had already backslapped his way onto the board of directors. But he was also the current club champion, which gave him a certain standing. Jimmy had no problem with that—he'd played a couple of rounds with Teddy and knew what a great shot maker he was. But there were other dimensions of Teddy's personality that Jimmy didn't care for.

For one thing, he happened to know that Teddy carried a nine-shot .22 pistol in his golf bag.

For another, Jimmy understood why.

Teddy was more a gambler than a golfer. He had a reputation for sandbagging—turning in high scores to run his handicap up—then conning his foursome into a high-stakes game. His standard bet was fifty dollars a hole, double on birdies, plus carry-overs on all ties. Guys could drop a thousand bucks in games like that and never know what hit them. That left more than a few people unhappy, which was bad for the general atmosphere of the club. But what made it worse was that Teddy tended to cheat. Nobody ever mentioned it, though, not to his face, because he also had a short fuse. Most of the locals had simply stopped playing with him. Still, around the clubhouse Teddy Mumford was a bulldozer of friendliness, and the people who didn't know him invariably liked him a lot.

Jimmy set the bucket aside and pulled open the front door. It was Mumford, all right, dressed in a white double-breasted suit and grinning like a long-lost relative. Moths flitted around his shoulders as if he were a source of light. A man and a woman stood behind him on the porch, but it was too dark for Jimmy to make out their faces. The man, he could tell, was pretty big.

"Jimmy-Boy! I knew you'd still be around." Teddy sounded even more jovial than usual.

"I'm washing the floor," Jimmy said, hoping that might relieve him of the obligation to invite anyone inside.

"Take a break," Teddy told him. "I want you to meet a couple of friends of mine." He reached out and rattled the aluminum storm door again. Jimmy had no choice but to unlock it.

Teddy stepped quickly inside and put his arm around Jimmy's shoulder. "A rock and a hard place," he said under his breath, and Jimmy had a vague sense that Mumford was apologizing for something that hadn't happened yet. "Jimmy Wickerham," he said, turning his smile to the couple now coming through the doorway, "this is Bill Rohrbaugh and his daughter, Willa. Bill was my partner in the tournament this weekend."

"Right, I remember," Jimmy said. "You bought a T-Line putter from me this morning."

A warm smile spread across Bill Rohrbaugh's weathered face. "Best investment I've made in years."

Jimmy wiped his wet palm on the side of his jeans and shook the man's outstretched hand. "Glad to meet you," he said, and then nodded politely to Willa. She seemed to be about his age, maybe a year older, and she smiled at him with a look of honest relief. Jimmy could understand that well enough: she'd probably spent the last two hours chewing dried-out chicken wings and watching a platoon of double-knit geezers do the polka.

"Jimmy's a great kid," Teddy announced, and playfully roughed his hair as if he were a favorite dog. Jimmy felt his face go red— he was too old to put up with that kind of condescending lock-er-room horseshit—but he knew better than to say anything. Willa was a good-looking girl, and he didn't want to rock the boat until he found out what the situation was.

"I hope you've had a good weekend," he said.

Mr. Rohrbaugh pulled a handkerchief from his pants pocket and blew his nose. "The golf was great," he said. Then he turned to Teddy and started to say something else, but Willa cut him off.

"The rest of it's been pretty dismal," she said, crossing her arms over her breasts. Jimmy nodded and smiled. Her dress was the bare-shoulder kind he thought was pretty hot, and it was low-cut enough to show the tan lines from her swimsuit. Her long hair had a silky look, and though the color might have seemed a dreary dishwa-ter blonde on someone else, on her it seemed radiant, not the least bit drab, each strand holding the light in a summertime chlorine glow. Her skin and teeth were flawless, which meant either good genes or good money—though genes were the long shot, given Bill Rohrbaugh's sagging bulk and the liver spots strung across his balding scalp. The only thing that kept Willa from seeming incredibly beautiful was that her father was standing next to her, demonstrating how ugly certain of her features might someday turn out to be. But that was natural: fathers could put anyone in a bad light; Jimmy knew that well enough. Her nose might eventually broaden into her old man's terrier look, and when she hit middle age, she might be in line for about sixty of his extra pounds. But that didn't matter. On this balmy clear night she looked like a prom queen's prom queen, even under the fluorescent lights, and it crossed Jimmy's mind, as it always did when he met a new girl or played a new course, that the world was full of possibility.

"Do you folks live around here?" He'd intended the question as an icebreaker for Willa, but it was her father who stepped in with the answer.

"We're from up at Lock Haven," he said. "I'm the human resources director at Continental Containers." He scanned the room for a moment, then pointed to the stack of new golf shoes beneath the windows. "That's one of our products right there."

"What? The Foot Joys?"

Mr. Rohrbaugh frowned. "No, not the shoes, the boxes. We make the packaging other companies put their products in. Everything from furniture crates to milk cartons. You name it, we've got a box for it."

"Listen," Teddy said, resting a hand on Mr. Rohrbaugh's round shoulder, "I've got to get a couple of things from my golf bag. Why don't you two browse around. If you see anything you like, Jimmy'll put it on my tab."

Mr. Rohrbaugh frowned. "I told you, I've got no interest in merchandise."

"I could use a sweater," Willa said, rubbing her hands up the backs of her arms. "It's chillier than I thought it would be."

"We're in a hollow," Jimmy explained. "There's a creek along the low side of the parking lot, and that cools the air down quicker. It's usually about five degrees colder here at night than it is in town."

Willa looked at him and smiled, but it was the smile of a tourist taking in the local color, and he felt his heart tighten.

"Fine, then," Mr. Rohrbaugh said. "My daughter'll take a sweater, and we'll knock off thirty bucks."

"They're thirty-eight dollars," Jimmy said, pointing to the shelf of women's sweaters along the rear wall. "But the register's already closed out."

"I said he could put it on my tab." Teddy's smile was so strained he looked demented. "You can write it up tomorrow."

Jimmy shrugged. "If you say so."

"Good man," said Teddy, clapping his hands together. He glanced around the room as if he were trying to remember what to do next, and suddenly Jimmy was able to read just how drunk Teddy was. Not sloppy, but exuberant—slightly out of control. Jimmy had seen him this way before, and knew it was best not to cross him. After a couple of vodka tonics Teddy tended to take an even narrower view of the world than usual, sizing up the people around him as either best friends or mortal enemies, with little ground in between.

"That's right, your golf was great," Teddy said. He leveled a look at Jimmy. "We won the goddamn tournament—did you know that? The whole shebang. They gave us each a new set of woods and two dozen golf balls."

"Yeah, I heard about it. Congratulations."

"Old Bill here couldn't miss a putt all day with that new T-Line you sold him. Best he's ever played in his life. Isn't that right, Bill?"

"I had the touch, all right."

Teddy leaned in close and tapped Jimmy in the chest with his forefinger. "The last hole: Bill knocks in a thirty-footer, and bingo! We beat out old man Guise and that bald-ass partner of his by one stroke. Guise was so mad he didn't know whether to shit or go blind." He paused to let this information sink in, and the four of them stood there in an awkward silence. It was the first time Jimmy had ever seen Teddy Mumford run a conversation into a concrete wall. Teddy seemed to notice it, too, and stared self-consciously at the floor between them. Then regaining his bearings, he snapped his head up and smiled. "Be right back," he said, and disappeared into the bag room.

"Well," said Jimmy, trying to pick up the slack, "I guess you guys made out okay."

Mr. Rohrbaugh blew his nose again, then folded the handkerchief neatly into quarters and tucked it into the breast pocket of his blazer. "Can't complain," he said.

Willa shook her head. "Well, I sure can." She turned abruptly and started toward the stack of women's sweaters.

"Willa's a little miffed," Mr. Rohrbaugh told him. "We were gonna check out some of the local colleges while we were here— that's why she came down with me. She hasn't been too happy up at State. But the tournament took more time than I thought, so we never got around to it."

"We could have skipped those stupid corndogs at the snack bar," Willa said over her shoulder.

"She's right about that," he conceded. "We both had stomach pains all night long. I almost didn't play today."

"Are these all you've got?" she asked, holding up one of the lavender pullovers. "I'd rather have one with buttons."

"Sorry," Jimmy said. "That's all we've got."

Teddy leaned his head through the bag room doorway. "Jimmy, could you give me a hand here. I can't find my golf bag."

"It's in your cubbyhole," Jimmy told him. "Top row, fourth from the right."

Teddy stared at him coldly. "Maybe you could show me."

Jimmy excused himself and followed Teddy back into the bag room, which was remarkably uncluttered considering the chaos of the last three days. There were still a few guests' golf bags crowded against the work table, but all the members' clubs and bags had already been cleaned and put away. Jimmy had done most of the work himself, so he wasn't surprised to see that Teddy's bag was exactly where it was supposed to be. "There you go," he said, pointing to the cubbyhole.

Teddy didn't even glance at his bag. He carefully closed the door and listened for a moment at the jamb, then turned to Jimmy and beamed his standard ingratiating smile. "You're invited to a party," he said.

There was something odd in Mumford's tone, some twist of attitude Jimmy couldn't quite identify, and it left him feeling disoriented, as if he'd used the wrong iron for a routine shot. He had no desire to get tangled up in this volatile drunk's rat-brained plans; but he also had no desire to lose his job. It was a bad idea to disappoint a board member, especially a vindictive jerk like Teddy Mumford.

And there was also Willa to consider. She smelled like air-conditioned flowers, perfect for the summer night, and he wouldn't mind a chance to make some kind of impression, even with her father hanging around. "When?" he asked.

"Now. Tonight."

"I've still got to wash the floor."

"That can wait." Teddy stepped in close to him. "Look, I'm not talking about some country club polka-fest. This guy I know is having a birthday bash up at his cabin on South Mountain. And he's hired a real band."

"Who?"

Mumford reached up and tightened the knot on his tie. "You don't know him."

"No, I mean who's the band?"

"The Radio Actives. I hear they're the best in the area."

Jimmy laughed. He'd heard the Radio Actives a couple of times around town. The guy on the lead guitar had a few good riffs, but the drummer and the bass player were both lousy and the guy on keyboards couldn't keep his equipment from shorting out. "They're totally lame," he said. "Except for a couple of old Beatles songs, all they do is country western."

Teddy took out his wallet and held it open. "You see this?" he asked, shaking it upside down to demonstrate its emptiness. "This is a major business problem."

Jimmy looked at the wallet. It was one of the most ornate he'd ever seen—new hand-tooled leather with a scene of stampeding horses embossed across the back and bits of polished turquoise mounted into the corners, each stone held in place by delicate silver brackets. The whole wallet bulged with business or credit cards and, even without cash, looked healthier than Jimmy's own billfold, which at the moment contained five dollars, a driver's license, and a YMCA pass. "I hope you're not asking me for a loan," he said.

Teddy waved his hand between them as if he were clearing away smoke. "Christ, no, that's not what I meant. I just want you to drive us to the party."

"Why me? Why don't you drive yourself?'

Teddy looked annoyed. "Because I'm drunk, for one thing. Any moron can see that." He took a deep breath and closed his eyes. "Anyway, you're a good kid and I'd like to have you along. You can keep what's-her-name entertained while I talk business with Bill. That shouldn't be such a chore." He opened his eyes and sagged back against a line of golf bags. Some loose clubs at the end of the row clanked against the sink and rattled to the floor, but Teddy didn't seem to notice. "Besides, you've got one of those Jeep four-wheel-drive things, don't you?"

"I've got an old Bronco."

"Perfect. This guy's cabin is out in the boonies, and his driveway is a little on the rough side. With all the rain we had last week, I don't think my Cadillac could handle the ruts."

"So skip it. Take them somewhere else. What's the big deal about a birthday party in the woods?"

Teddy glanced toward the door and lowered his voice to a hoarse whisper. "The big deal is that the birthday guy owes me fifteen hundred bucks, and I need it right now." He grabbed Jimmy by the front of his sweatshirt and tugged him a step closer. "Bill Rohrbaugh assigns the insurance contracts at Continental Containers, and I can't let him leave town thinking I'm too broke to cover my gambling debts. That's a bad image for business."

"You mean you bet against your own partner?"

Teddy released his grip on the sweatshirt and frowned. "There's no such thing as partners," he said. "Now are you gonna drive us up there or not?"

The trip took longer than Teddy said it would. He claimed he'd been to the cabin twice before, but never at night, and now, cursing the pitch-black mountain roads, he had trouble recognizing landmarks. Jimmy was reasonably familiar with the area—he'd attended church camp in these woods one summer when he was twelve, right after his mother died—but none of the roads or driveway entrances were marked with anything more revealing than occasional blue or red reflector discs, so he had to rely on Teddy's sense of direction. At each trail that split from the main road, Teddy leaned out his window to scrutinize the invisible landscape, claimed a flicker of recognition, then reversed himself and told Jimmy to drive on.

After half a dozen of these false alarms, Teddy suddenly said "Stop here!" with an urgency that made Jimmy think they'd found the spot at last. But then Teddy stuck his head out into the cool night air and vomited down the side of the Bronco. Jimmy figured that would probably bring the evening to a close, but Mr. Rohrbaugh had apparently nodded off at some point along the way and had no complaints about the change in Teddy's condition.

"I get carsick when I ride in back," Teddy explained, then stumbled from the car into the edge of the dark woods.

"I think we've got a couple of drunks on our hands," Willa said, though she didn't seem upset. Jimmy listened to the soft snoring of Mr. Rohrbaugh in the back seat.

"I thought your father was pretty sober," Jimmy whispered.

"If he were sober we wouldn't be here. But people kept buying him drinks all night because he won the tournament."

"He sure holds it well."

"Only up to a point," she said. "Then he goes down like he got hit with a tranquilizer dart."

"That's not a bad way to be," he said, thinking of the times his own father had drunk too much in public. Willa seemed genuinely at ease with her father's present state, even amused by it, and that was an attitude he simply couldn't fathom. Maybe it meant she had the warmest heart he'd ever come across, or maybe it meant she had no heart at all.

Teddy lunged from the black weeds back to the side of the Bronco and leaned his head through the rear window. "We're there," he said. "I can hear the music."

Jimmy turned off the motor and listened. The faint strains of an electric guitar filtered up through the woods on their right. Or maybe it wasn't an electric guitar. The notes were so muffled and fragmented they might have come from any number of instruments—saxophones, fiddles, a synthesizer, even an accordion. It was music reduced to its most general form, a charming seepage of sounds with no melody, no rhythm, nothing but the loose wash of an undefined harmony weaving up through the trees. "I think it's coming from down there," he said, pointing into the darkness on Willa's side of the Bronco. "But it still sounds pretty far away."

"I remember now," said Teddy, climbing back inside. "That's the turn-off." He pointed to a pair of red reflectors glowing by the side of the road forty yards ahead.

Jimmy started the engine and eased the Bronco forward. "You still want to do this?" he asked Willa. "I mean, with your father asleep and all. . ."

"Hell, yes," she said brightly. "This is the most fun I've had all weekend."

Jimmy steered between the reflectors and nudged the Bronco over the packed arch of the shoulder. "I can't see what the driveway's like in front of us," he said. "The headlights are angled too high."

"Well, it's not actually a driveway," Teddy said. "It's sort of a trail the guy scraped out with a backhoe. It's basically just a couple of ruts, so take it easy going down."

Jimmy rode the brake hard as the Bronco groaned along the steep slope. Teddy had been right about the ruts, which were deep enough to scrape the front axle, but gravity and momentum kept the tires from spinning in the mud.

"We'll never get back up this hill," said Willa.

"No need to," Teddy told her. "This lane runs all the way through the property. It comes out on one of the county roads further down the mountain."

Jimmy kept his eyes on the narrow cut of trees ahead and wound the Bronco slowly down the switchback trail. After a few minutes the music grew more distinct, rising now above the noise of their engine, and Jimmy caught glimpses of lights flickering through the overgrown woods.

Willa suddenly put a hand on his shoulder. "Stop," she said. Jimmy jammed the brake and the Bronco skidded gently to a halt. "Look over there," she said, pointing into the trees on her side of the cut. Teddy leaned forward between the seats and the three of them stared out at the tangle of undergrowth. Twenty yards ahead, just inside the angle of the headlight beams, a cluster of tiny red lights glowed in the shadows.

"Those are eyes," said Teddy.

"A family of possums, most likely," Jimmy said. "Or maybe raccoons."

"Why are they all staring at us?" Willa asked. "Why don't they run away or hide or something."

"We're too scary to run from," Jimmy told her. "Instinct makes them keep an eye on whatever they think might be dangerous."

"He's right," said Teddy. "Watch this." He reached across to the steering wheel and honked the horn. None of the eyes moved. "I used to go night hunting this way," he went on. "What you do is go out into a clearing and lean on the horn a few times, then shine a light up into the trees. Whatever's up there'll be watching you, and the light reflects in their eyes. They won't even blink if they can help it. Then you just draw a bead and pop 'em right between the glow-spots."

Jimmy eased off the brake and let the Bronco roll forward. The family of eyes receded into the darkness. "It's illegal to hunt that way," he pointed out.

"True enough," said Teddy. "But it sure saves a lot of time and legwork."

"I know something about raccoons," Willa said. "When a baby raccoon cries, it sounds just like a human baby."

Teddy snorted and leaned farther forward. "I guess you picked that up at college."

Willa crossed her arms and stared straight ahead into the

flurry of moths batting through the high beams. "I'll tell you what I picked up at college—not a goddamn thing."

Teddy took a small tube of breath spray from his inside suit pocket and squirted a long stream into his mouth. "Well, I'll tell you what a baby raccoon sounds like because I know. It sounds like a goddamn baby raccoon."

Teddy's equilibrium was returning, but so was his native belligerence, and Jimmy began to scan the woods ahead for some timely distraction. "I think I see the band lights," he said, and it was true: as they rounded the final bend of the grade, the dense trees parted into a broad clearing. Forty yards to their left was the cabin, and beside it the elevated platform where the band, in a flood of colored lights, was now blasting its way through a frenzied version of an old Rolling Stones song. A hundred people, maybe more, danced wildly on a rocky patch of ground before the bandstand, some of the men without their shirts, and nearly everyone held large plastic drinking cups. Of those who weren't dancing, most clustered in smaller groups across the hillside, a few here by the fallen tree trunk, a few there on the cabin porch, some weaving in the shadows, searching, most likely, for bathrooms or beer. At least a dozen lay passed out or sleeping on a gallery of rough blankets spread against one bank of the clearing, their arms and legs splayed in every direction. Pickup trucks and ATVs littered the low end of the clearing, all crowded haphazardly along the side of the grade like shells in a junkyard. But the raw edge of the music carved its own electric space up through the tall cathedral of trees, and for a moment Jimmy felt overwhelmed by the spectacle. That so much color and sound and human celebration could take place in the middle of a darkened mountain forest seemed nothing short of miraculous. But at the same time he felt timid in the face of it all, an alien in an indecipherable landscape. How could people dance so hard where none of the ground was level?

"My God," said Willa. "I think we just found out what happened to the druids."

Teddy laughed and swung open the car door. "Park it anywhere," he said. "And if Bill wakes up, tell him to look for me at the cabin." He got out and started across the field, his white suit glowing in the headlights.

"If my Dad wakes up, he'll probably make us leave. I don't think this was the kind of party he was expecting." She pulled her new sweater down low over the front of her dress. "I wish

I'd worn jeans. I look like somebody's fairy godmother."

"I've got a sweat suit in the back," Jimmy told her. "You can wear that if you want."

"Great," she said.

Jimmy pulled the Bronco onto a firm stretch of shoulder and parked it. "It's in my golf bag," he said. "I'll go dig it out." He circled to the rear hatch and rummaged for the clothes. "I don't have any shoes for you," he said.

"I'll go barefoot."

He took out the rolled-up sweats and sniffed them. He'd worn them the day before to clean out a poison ivy patch between the fourth and fifth fairways, but they didn't seem too rank. He closed the hatch and climbed back into the Bronco. He'd already shut the door behind him before he realized Willa had taken off both her sweater and her dress and was sitting beside him now in nothing but her underpants and bra. At first he thought he should jump back out and apologize like some dumb kid, but that would have been too phony to stomach. His shyness had dried up long ago, and it took more than the sight of a little bare skin to sweep him into panic. He turned toward her on the seat and handed over the sweatsuit as casually as if he were selling her golf tees. For her part Willa didn't seem embarrassed at all, but Jimmy still felt uneasy. He couldn't tell if he were being brazenly rude or infinitely polite.

"Can you imagine if my Dad woke up right now?" she said, and Jimmy felt a shiver run through him. But Mr. Rohrbaugh was still slumped peacefully against the door frame, rattling out his deep, slow breaths. Willa quickly slipped the sweatshirt over her head and shook out the bottoms by the waistband. "Which is crazy, really," she went on, shoving her feet awkwardly down the pant legs. "I mean, he wouldn't think twice if I was sitting here in a bikini. Why do you suppose that is?"

"It's just part of the rulebook," Jimmy said. "Some things are out of bounds."

"You're cute," she said, and got out of the Bronco.

Jimmy followed her across the clearing to the fringes of the dance crowd. The band had now launched into a bone-jarring attack on a recent top-forty tune he'd once liked but had finally grown sick of. The sound of it moved right through him, tangible and rude, like a current too strong to resist. Still, it was an opportunity, so he touched Willa's arm to ask her to dance.

She smiled sourly and shook her head, then circled slowly away from him toward the side of the stage. Jimmy trailed after her, though he wondered if maybe she wanted him to get lost.

When she reached the corner of the risers, Willa put her hands over her ears and stepped directly in front of the amplifier. Then she turned toward him, letting the volume pound against her back. She called out something to him, but it was lost in the thunder of the music.

The band was better than he remembered. The guy on keyboards had apparently learned how to hook up his equipment without blowing a speaker, and he played now in a cool balance between abandon and control. The vocalist was new—a redhead with a voice like polished glass, and Jimmy could see from the slink of her gown that the band was tinkering with its image, moving away from country western into something with an even deeper ache, a little closer to mainstream, maybe, but still desperately fatal, as if each wailing note might be their last.

As he moved in closer, Willa stepped away from the amp and they walked together toward the back edge of the clearing, where an enormous fallen tree sloped upward into the darkness.

"It was like taking a shower," she said happily.

"What was?"

"Standing in front of the speaker like that. I could really feel it." She glanced at him sideways. "Better than cocaine," she said.

"I wouldn't know."

She sat back against the ragged trunk. "Well, I would. That's why I'm in the market for a new college."

"You got kicked out for doing drugs?"

"I got hospitalized for doing drugs. Now my dad figures I need a different environment."

"What happened?"

"Nothing very dramatic. I mean I wasn't trying to kill myself or anything. I just screwed up. Big weekend, lots of parties—I drank too much beer one night and then hooked up with some friends who had some better coke than I was used to. For a while I really thought I was gonna die."

"Sounds pretty scary."

"Yeah, it was. I never passed out, I just kept getting colder and colder. It was like I could feel my whole body shutting down, piece by piece, and there was no way to stop it. I had to concentrate as hard as I could just to keep breathing. But I knew if I could ride it out long enough I'd be okay." She smiled at him and spread her palms. "And here I am, back on the old dance floor. No particular damage."

"I'm glad," he said lamely.

The drummer broke into a staccato burst that punctuated the end of their song, and the redheaded singer mumbled into the microphone that the Radio Actives were through for the night. A chorus of protests rose from the dance crowd, but the musicians had already begun to disconnect their equipment, oblivious, it seemed, to their own popularity.

Willa swung a leg up and straddled the tree trunk. "Your turn," she said. "Tell me something true."

"No lobster ever makes it out of Iowa alive."

Willa shook her head and pulled a brittle strip of bark from the tree. "You're a disappointment," she said. She climbed carefully to her feet and began to walk away from him along the angle of the trunk.

"I wouldn't go barefoot on this tree if I were you," he said. "We get a lot of black widows in these parts."

She stopped about ten steps up the angle and casually scanned the bark around her feet. "I'm not too concerned. Statistics are on my side." She smiled down at him and started to say something more, but the look on her face suddenly darkened, and for a second Jimmy thought she'd actually been bitten.

"What's the matter?" he asked.

Willa descended the trunk and stepped gingerly into the dirt beside him. "Trouble in paradise," she said, staring past him toward the cabin. He turned in time to see Mumford sailing like a half-folded sheet from the elevated porch, clearing the steps altogether and landing hard on his side in the rocky yard. "Ouch," said Willa, but there was something like a laugh in her voice, and Jimmy realized how tough she was.

He took her hand and they started together toward Mumford, who rolled onto his back and slowly pushed himself up by his elbows. A shirtless man in blue jeans and work boots stepped to the edge of the porch and folded his arms across his sunburned chest. He wasn't big, but he was muscular, with a loose, hardened look about him, as if he worked on road crews, maybe, or in rock quarries, running heavy equipment.

The fight, if that's what it had been, was apparently over, since Mumford seemed in no particular hurry to pick himself up from the dirt. Even so, Jimmy knew better than to barge too clumsily into the aftermath.

"Hi, Teddy," he said as he and Willa made their way up beside him in the yard. "How's it going?" The man on the porch sized Jimmy up and dismissed him in a single flick of the eye. Then he turned his glare back on Mumford, who ran his fingers nonchalantly through his hair and squinted over his shoulder toward the band.

"At the moment," he said, "I have no opinion."

The man on the porch walked heavily down the steps. "Don't expect to get your hardware back," he said, pointing a thick finger at Mumford's face. "And don't you ever pull a stunt like that around me again." Then he climbed back up the steps, taking them two at a time, and disappeared into the cabin.

"Looks like you took a bad spill," Jimmy said as he helped Mumford to his feet.

"Yeah. It's a good thing I'm drunk, or I mighta got hurt," he said, smiling and straightening his tie. He brushed clumsily at the dirt caked on the right side of his pants, then wiped a trickle of blood from his nose onto his white coat sleeve. "I'll probably have to get this dry cleaned," he said, fingering a tear in the breast pocket.

"What was that all about?" Willa asked. "Who was that guy?"

Mumford shrugged. "Just some guy." Then he looked around slowly, scrutinizing the trees. "You know, I don't think this is the right party after all."

The three of them walked across the noisy clearing, weaving their way through scores of drunken lovers, stopping periodically for Mumford to tilt his head back in an effort to stanch his nosebleed. As they neared the Bronco, Mumford lurched ahead and peered in the window at Willa's father, who was still sleeping comfortably in the back seat. Jimmy put a hand on Mumford's shoulder to guide him clear of the door, but Mumford shook it off and stumbled toward the rear of the Bronco. "You kids go back to the party," he said, sitting awkwardly on the corner of the bumper. "I'm still a little woozy from that fall. If it's all the same to you, I'm not up to a buggy ride just yet." He closed his eyes and leaned slowly forward, cupping his head in his hands. "Just give me twenty minutes, and I'll be fine."

Jimmy turned to Willa, but she was already walking away. He followed her down past the bandstand to the edge of the trees and caught up with her at the fallen trunk.

"I don't know what to say," he told her.

She nodded. "A lot goes on." Then she surprised him with a smile. "You're a golfer, right? Say something about that. Tell me your most glorious golf story."

A tiredness fell across him like a wave, and he sat back against the rough slope of the trunk. "I don't have one," he told her.

"Oh, come on. All golfers have golf stories. My father's no good at all, but even he comes home every week with some golf miracle he's just dying to talk about. Did you ever win any big tournaments?"

"No," he said, and for the first time it came to him that he probably never would.

"Ever come close?"

"Once, I guess. Three years ago in the state juniors championship. I blew a three-stroke lead on the final hole."

"Did you come in second?"

"I didn't come in at all. I was disqualified."

"What was it—did they catch you cheating?"

Jimmy laughed. "No, nothing like that. It was stupid. I got into a fistfight with my caddie and never finished the round."

Willa sat beside him on the trunk. "Why'd you do that?"

Jimmy shrugged. "He handed me the wrong club. I guess I got mad."

Willa giggled and took him by the arm. "You're a dangerous character," she said.

He decided to let it go at that. There was no sense dragging up any more of the story than he had to—no need to tell her that the caddie was his father, or that his father was a violent alcoholic who had drunk himself nearly into a stupor by the eighteenth hole. Willa's father was harmless—a gentle snoring businessman who'd had a few too many; she might not understand the kind of timber rattler other drunks could be.

Teddy Mumford was a rattler in the making. He'd pushed his luck tonight, and that had clearly caused him some damage—but he probably hadn't learned anything. Mumford was a guy with a wrong attitude, and even if it didn't get him killed tonight, it surely would someday.

But he knew Willa was right—in his own way he was every bit as dangerous a character as Teddy Mumford. He didn't drink or smoke or gamble or do drugs, but that didn't mean much: there were far more serious dependencies to wrestle with. Even now there was a ticking in his chest he couldn't answer.

"This is nice," he said quietly, and Willa leaned her head against his shoulder. They sat for a long moment staring into the black curtain of the woods, propping each other up like tired players at the end of a season.

Behind them the band continued packing up its gear, and he heard someone offer five hundred dollars if they'd stay for another set. "We've got people waiting at home" was the only reply.

Jimmy thought of the graffiti he'd scrubbed this morning from the bathroom stalls in the men's locker room. Most of it had been the same standard ugly stuff he'd seen in public restrooms everywhere—in high schools, bus depots, and restaurants: nothing clean and nothing memorable. But today he'd found one happy declaration scratched into the paint of the lavatory door. *I kissed a girl,* it read.

I kissed a girl.

The pathetic innocence of that line amazed him. *I kissed a girl,* as if some poor boy's life had suddenly found the order he had dreamed of, as if the future extended from that moment only, as if tenderness were something strong enough to last.

I kissed a girl, as if something that small were all it took to save someone.

Such unschooled hope was downright staggering, and remembering it now, even with Willa pressing a soft cheek against his sleeve, he had to think hard not to cry.

ONCE UPON A TIME, A SCAVENGER

His mama said anything he found he could keep.

It was like a big treasure hunt. God had sent a strong wind to take things away from the stores and hide them all over the countryside. Some things might be broken, but other things might be good as new. If Jerry Lee found something he liked, he could put it in his wagon and bring it home with him.

The idea of it amazed him. He might find all the toys he'd ever wanted. Red rubber balls or toy hammers or slide whistles or tops or cat's eye marbles. There might be toy soldiers that he could send out on patrol and pretend that one of them was his brother, Web. He might even find his favorite, the wooden gliders that cost a nickel at the Rea & Derrick.

But his mama also told him to remember his family. He should leave room in his wagon for gifts, because God's blessings should always be shared. So if he found clothes that weren't his size, or things for the kitchen, or ashtrays, or anything else good for grown-ups, he should gather those up, too, for his cousins and his aunts and uncles and his grandma. Maybe he could even find something to give his daddy for his birthday, she had told him.

He'd only been searching for a little while, and already he'd found a lamp that was broken in half but that still had good wires in it. He'd also found a broken picture frame with a color picture of a collie in it, and a bedsheet that was heavier than it looked because it came out of the creek. If his mama didn't want the bedsheet, he'd use it for his costume next Halloween.

He found a tire that his daddy might like, but it was too big to put in the wagon. Maybe Jerry Lee could come back for it later. But he also found a brand-new fancy shoe like his daddy wore sometimes when he and mama went out in the evenings. *Wingtips,* his daddy called them, even though they didn't have any wings. This one looked real nice—shiny and black with stitches sewn all over it. Maybe he'd even find the other shoe that went with it. But it would still be a good gift, even if he didn't. One shoe was better than no shoe; Jerry Lee had learned that much already.

There were also plenty of boards with good nails in them, but the ones that weren't broken were too long to carry. Besides, these boards probably came from the new house they were building down the street from his mama and daddy's place, and it wasn't right to take things that belonged to a neighbor.

The toys were harder to find than he thought they would be. In his mind, he'd seen them hanging from tree branches like it was Christmas morning, low enough that he could walk right up and pick them, easy as crabapples. He did see some things in trees, but they were too high up, and anyway he couldn't tell for sure what they were. They might have been parts of houses, and he didn't think his mama needed anything like that.

Still, he would keep looking. There might be grand surprises in the tall grass further along the creek bank toward the river, and today was finders-keepers day.

He stood at the crest of the higher bank beside his half-full wagon and scanned the creek bed for more presents. Something caught his eye downstream, something lodged in the mud at the mouth of the culvert. He left his wagon and walked a few steps closer, squinting hard to make out what it was. When it finally came into focus, his heart leapt and he broke into a run along the rocky bank.

It was a catcher's mitt, the kind he'd seen in the window at Malone Hardware. Maybe it was the very same one. And there was no one else around to call dibs. The mitt was his alone.

He knelt in the rocky mud at the outer rim of the concrete tunnel that ran under the roadway, and pulled the mitt from the tangle of mud and weeds. Even dirty, it still smelled brand-new, and it was so stiff he could hardly bend it, even with both hands. Neatsfoot oil, that's what he needed to loosen it up. Web had told him that was how to make a baseball glove soft—

soak it in Neatsfoot oil and tie it shut overnight with a baseball tucked in the pocket. He didn't know what Neatsfoot oil was, but he knew his daddy could find some.

Jerry Lee scraped most of the mud off with his finger and slid his hand into the opening. His fingers were too short to reach all the way inside, but that was all right, he was growing every day, that's what his mama told him. He pounded his fist into the pocket, the way he had seen Web do when Web and his daddy had thrown the hard ball around in the chicken yard. It stung his fingers, but that was all right, too. Big boys didn't mind if something hurt a little bit.

Web had taken their ball with him to the army, so Jerry Lee would have to get himself another one. But maybe he'd find a ball today, too. Then he could take Web's place with his daddy in the chicken yard, and his daddy could cheer up again.

He tucked the mitt up under his arm and began to look around for other windfalls. Almost right away he spotted something. Not four feet away, just inside the edge of the concrete tunnel, partly hidden by weeds and a chunk of concrete, was another shoe. He could only see part of it, but he could tell it didn't match the wingtip he'd already collected. This one was a dark brown instead of black, and it didn't look very new at all. Still, two shoes were better than one, no matter what they looked like.

He clapped his hands loudly to scare away any snakes or rats that might be waiting in the dark crevices beneath the tunnel and scooted down the bank to the lower edge of the culvert. He couldn't climb inside the tunnel very easily without stepping in the creek, and he didn't want to do that. He was barefooted, and there were crawfish under the rocks, sometimes as big as his hand, with pincers strong enough to make him bleed. Besides, this early in the year the water was still too cold for wading.

He set the mitt carefully on the curve of dry cement at the top of the arch, then gripped the side of the tunnel and leaned out across the dark opening. He felt a little uneasy because he didn't know what kinds of things lived in tunnels under the road. Maybe bears. Or bobcats. Maybe wild dogs, like Rufus. His mother had told him to stay away from wild dogs because they might have rabies. Rabies meant you foamed at the mouth and went crazy and were afraid of water. If Rufus lived here, though, he couldn't have rabies, because there was water all around. And Rufus wasn't as bad as his mother thought, anyway.

Jerry Lee told her he had walked right up and patted his head once, and Rufus hadn't minded. His daddy had laughed when he said that, but told him he was brave.

He needed to be brave now, too. He reached out as far as he could and hooked the heel of the shoe with his fingertips. He tried to pull it toward him, but it seemed to be caught on something. He tugged harder to try to break the snag, but the shoe still wouldn't budge, so he edged closer and reached across the shoe-top for a better grip. But as he closed his fingers over the tightly strung laces, he suddenly understood something, and a terrible fear squeezed him from inside. He froze. The shoe was hard to move because it wasn't empty. There was a foot in it, and probably a leg beyond that, stretching off into the darkness of the tunnel. Jerry Lee had grabbed hold of something straight from his worst nightmares, the ones where Jesus didn't save him from the Enemy. And now he was too afraid to let go.

But he didn't have to let go. The shoe pulled away from him all by itself, and a sorrowful moan rose up inside the tunnel, echoing louder than what any normal person ever sounded like, more like a monster waking up. Jerry Lee sprang backward and scrambled up over the top of the culvert to the gravel surface of the road. Whatever it was, it was now directly beneath him.

It moaned again. Jerry Lee crept back to the edge of the culvert and snatched up his new catcher's mitt and held it to his heart. He didn't know what to do next. If he ran for his wagon, he'd have to go back along the creek bank, and the thing in the tunnel could see him. Maybe if he just stayed where he was, he'd be safe.

But what kind of monster moaned so much and wore brown shoes?

In the story of the Three Billy Goats Gruff, the billy goats had a bad troll under their road. He didn't know exactly what a troll was, but in the picture book it didn't wear shoes. Maybe that didn't mean anything, though. He remembered that all the goats were smarter than the bad troll, and so it hadn't been able to win. And Jerry Lee was even smarter than goats, he knew that for a fact. They were dumb enough to eat tin cans. So maybe he didn't have as much to be afraid of as he thought.

Still.

His mama had promised him there was no such thing as trolls, and his daddy had said he shouldn't believe in any of that kind of stuff—not in trolls or fairies or goblins or Paul Bunyan or the Wolf Man or even haints.

But the Tooth Fairy had already brought him a nickel three times. Every year the Easter Bunny left colored eggs out in the yard, and that was sure no regular bunny. Reverend Johnson warned them every Sunday about the Devil, and all the magic tricks he used to catch their souls. Santa Claus had to be some kind of haint, floating up and down chimneys the way he did. And Jesus was definitely a haint because he was the Holy Ghost.

Maybe some people didn't believe in things like that unless they saw it for themselves. Daddy said Web was gone, that the Enemy got him, but Mama still talked to Web at night sometimes, and to Jesus, too. So he knew his mama believed in haints, no matter what his daddy had to say about it. And if Web was a haint now, then Jerry Lee believed in them, too.

So there was no telling what this thing under the road might be.

It moaned again, and then Jerry Lee thought he heard it call out something in a nearly normal voice, though he couldn't make out the words. Somehow the thing didn't sound as scary now. It didn't sound mad, it sounded more like it was hurt, like it needed help. He remembered a story about a little boy who pulled a thorn out of a lion's paw, and then the lion was his friend forever. Maybe he could do something like that, too.

He got down on his hands and knees and crawled quietly to the edge of the culvert. He leaned his head out far enough to see the brown shoe near the mouth of the tunnel. The shoe was right where he'd left it, but now the tunnel was filled with a groaning noise that went up and down, like the way his grandma breathed.

"Who's there?" Jerry Lee asked. The groaning noise stopped.

"Who's there yourself?" The voice was deep and ragged, and after it finished the question, it went into a harsh cough.

Jerry Lee didn't want to say who he was, so he tried to think of a way around it.

"I believe in Jesus," Jerry Lee answered.

There was a silence, followed by a shifting around inside the tunnel. Maybe Jerry Lee had found the Enemy, and it was about to come after him. The Enemy didn't like Jesus. His daddy had said so.

"Me, too, I reckon," said the voice. "Washed in the blood of the lamb," it added, which was the same thing Reverend Johnson said sometimes. Jerry Lee didn't know what it meant, exactly. But he knew it was supposed to be a good thing, even though it sounded awful.

Jerry Lee decided to take a risk.

"I'm Jerry Lee Statten," he announced, as boldly as he could speak it.

There was another silence.

"I know some Stattens," the voice said at last. "You any kin to Sammy Statten, up on Reservoir Hill?"

This caught him off guard.

"That's my daddy," Jerry Lee said.

"Well, your daddy's a good man," said the voice. "He's had a tough row to hoe here lately. I guess you all have."

Jerry Lee climbed down the side of the culvert and peered around into the tunnel. It took a little while for his eyes to see in the darkness, but what he finally saw made him somehow happy and frightened at the same time. Leaning back against the curve of the concrete wall was a man with only one leg.

"You're Mr. Gatlin," he whispered. Everybody knew of Mr. Gatlin. He was the only one-legged man in town.

"Reckon that's right," said Mr. Gatlin. He looked around and scooted further up the wall, dragging his leg out of the trickle of water in the bottom of the tunnel. "Where exactly are we right now?" he asked.

"Under Mulberry Avenue," Jerry Lee told him. "In the creek."

"Norris Creek? Down by Roy Hopkins' filling station?"

"I don't know," said Jerry Lee. "There's an Esso station."

"That's the one," said Mr. Gatlin. He wiped his shirt sleeve across his brow. "I don't guess you'd happen to know how I got here," he said.

Jerry Lee didn't want to answer, because Mr. Gatlin might take it as bad news. But it was too big a thing to lie about.

"You got killed by the tornado," he said. "Everybody said so. They found your wooden leg on the town square."

Another silence.

Mr. Gatlin cleared his throat and spit something out onto the tunnel floor. "No wonder I'm feeling poorly," he said, and he started to cough in a way that sounded like laughing.

"You was digging a well for Dr. McKinney," Jerry Lee went on.

"I remember that part," said Mr. Gatlin, "and I seem to recall being mashed by a tree. But the rest is all God's mystery." Then Mr. Gatlin twisted his body a little so he was facing Jerry

Lee straight on. "There was other folks with me. Did anybody else get hurt?"

Jerry Lee heard something that sounded like worry, or maybe even fear, in Mr. Gatlin's voice, but he knew that couldn't be right. Haints had nothing to be afraid of.

"No, sir," he answered. "Lots of things got broken, but you was the only one got killed."

Mr. Gatlin let out a raspy sigh, then fell into another silence.

Jerry Lee stepped carefully into the mouth of the tunnel and squatted against the wall across from Mr. Gatlin. He waited there in the quiet, with his baseball mitt clutched to his chest, listening to Mr. Gatlin breathe. After a while, he saw Mr. Gatlin's eyes shining in the shadows.

"I see you're a ball player," Mr. Gatlin said.

"Yes, sir. When I get big I'm going to play for the Brooklyn Dodgers."

"Like Jackie Robinson," said Mr. Gatlin. "I hear he's the highest-paid player on the team."

"He's the best," Jerry Lee told him.

"Well, your brother was mighty good," said Mr. Gatlin. "No reason you can't be, too."

"I don't have a ball," he said.

"That's not a problem. I never had me a ball neither. Used to play catch with hedge apples. You ever try that?"

"I roll them down the hill sometimes," said Jerry Lee.

"That's fun, too," Mr. Gatlin agreed. He winced as he shifted his weight onto his side. Then he leaned his head forward into the light and spit something dark into the creek. Jerry Lee felt bad seeing what shape he was in. He looked like he had rust spots all over him, on his face, down his neck, even in his hair. His shirt collar had rust spots, too, and his sleeves were crusty with mud and with the chalky white dust from the cement walls. Mr. Gatlin looked at Jerry Lee like he could tell what he was thinking.

"I guess I must look pretty stove up," he said.

"Yes, sir."

"I'll tell you the truth, Jerry Lee," he said, propping himself on his forearm. "I feel stove up, too. That twister was rough as a cob."

"Rough as Jersey Joe Walcott," Jerry Lee said.

Mr. Gatlin nodded and smiled. "You know about Jersey Joe, do you?"

"He's the champ. That means he can knock down anybody he wants." Jerry Lee pretended to scowl and swung his right arm in a small circle, delivering an uppercut to some invisible foe. "Jersey Joe's not afraid of anything."

Mr. Gatlin turned his face to the trickle of water and coughed hard. "That gives him a leg up on me," he said, wheezing out his words like there was a fish bone in his throat.

"I could get you an aspirin," Jerry Lee told him. "My mama keeps some in the medicine chest."

"That's a kind offer," said Mr. Gatlin. "But I've got my own aspirin at home. I just need to get there."

"Where do you live?" Jerry Lee asked.

"Not far." He reached down past the cement lip of the culvert and dipped his cupped hand into the creek. "You know where the stockyards are?" he asked, and splashed his face with water.

"I can hear the cows sometimes," Jerry Lee said.

"I've got a little place back of the holding pens," he said, wiping the drips from his stubbly chin. "On a normal day, I could just walk right over there. But today's not a normal day for me."

"No, sir,"

"You know why?"

Jerry Lee pointed to the place where Mr. Gatlin's right leg came to a sudden stop. "You missing your wooden leg today," he said.

Mr. Gatlin chuckled and nodded. "That's exactly the problem, Jerry Lee. But you could help me out, if you wanted to."

"You need my daddy's wheelbarrow?"

"Thank you, but I don't think that would do it." Mr. Gatlin squinted out at the creek bank. "Do you know what crutches are?"

"My Aunt Nelda got crutches when she stepped in a gopher hole."

"Well, that's what I need."

"But she lives in Skinum," Jerry Lee told him.

"That's all right, son, it doesn't have to be those particular crutches." He waved his hand at the opening of the tunnel. "I suspect there's a whole mess of fallen tree branches out there. Is that right?"

"Yes, sir."

"Well, I need you to drag one down here. The biggest you can handle. One with a fork in it about yea high." He held his hand up to the concrete ceiling, taller than Jerry Lee's head. "You understand?"

"Yes, sir." This was the part he'd been waiting for. The favor. He would do Mr. Gatlin this favor, and then Mr. Gatlin would always be on his side, always protect him from the Enemy. He stood on the lip of the culvert. "I'll get you a good one," he said, and jumped to the near bank. He didn't know why a haint needed a crutch to get home, but that part didn't matter. Maybe haints could only fly after dark. Or maybe this was just a test, something Mr. Gatlin made up so Jerry Lee could prove himself. He climbed quickly to the crest and ran to his wagon, where he tucked his catcher's mitt inside the wet bed sheet.

Mr. Gatlin was right, there were broken limbs everywhere. He ran from one to another, searching for the very best crutch. Most were too small, just spindly twigs with bunches of leaves. A few were too large, thicker than fence posts, and fanning out so wide he knew he could never drag them down to the culvert. Some looked good at first, stout and dark with no leaves at all, but those all ended up being rotten.

It was like the story of the Three Bears, where everything was either too much or too little, until something in-between showed up and turned out to be just right. That's what he needed now, the one that was in-between, and he knew it would be here some-where because that was the lesson of the story. He could always find the exact thing he needed if he looked hard enough. Just like he had found Mr. Gatlin.

He ran a little farther up the hill and climbed up onto the rock wall that ran along the back of the Crabtrees' yard, where he wasn't supposed to go. The Crabtrees had a little black-and-white dog with pointy ears and a flat nose that always barked and tried to snap at him when he came too close. But today it wasn't there. Maybe the tornado had got the Crabtrees' dog the same as it had got Mr. Gatlin.

From the top of the wall he could see all the fallen branches on the hillside. He cupped his hands around his eyes to block the sun, and stared hard at the piles of brush dotting the slope. None of the limbs looked right. He took a few steps along the wall and was about to hop back to the ground when he noticed a thick, forked branch poking from a bush beside the Crabtrees' back stoop. He couldn't be sure until he'd pulled it out, but it looked like the size Mr. Gatlin needed—thick as the neck of a baseball bat, but twice as long, with all the little branches broken off already. If it wasn't rotten, it would be just right for a crutch.

He jumped into the soft dirt of the flower bed and ran to the thick row of bushes along the back of the house. As he tugged at the stick, which was caught up somehow in the heart of the bush, he was startled by the sudden rapping at the kitchen window. It was unfriendly rapping, the kind that said, *Get out of my yard.*

Jerry Lee jerked hard at the stick, and as it broke free of the snag, he stumbled backward and tripped over the edge of one of the Crabtrees' sidewalk stones. He fell onto his backside just as the person who rapped on the window—Mrs. Crabtree, most likely, or maybe her maid—opened the door halfway. The little black-and-white dog burst through the opening and leapt from the concrete stoop toward Jerry Lee, snarling all the way. He tried to fend off the dog with his bare feet, kicking at its muzzle, but it was too quick for him, and before Jerry Lee could squirm away, the dog had bitten his foot and sunk its teeth in his leg, shaking its head back and forth and ripping the bluejeans that his cousin Arthur had just recently outgrown.

Jerry Lee grabbed up the perfect crutch and slammed it down on the dog's head. It let go of his leg and jumped sideways, yelping, and Jerry Lee hoped this was his chance to get away. He scrambled to his feet and hobbled backward toward the rock wall, still holding the crutch and keeping his eye on the dog, which was already shaking off its injury and growling louder than before.

"Sic him, Chester!" came a woman's voice from inside the darkness of the house, and the dog ran at him again. But this time Jerry Lee was better prepared, he had Mr. Gatlin's crutch to keep the dog away instead of just his bare feet, and he aimed the pointy end, the end where the branch had broken unevenly from the tree, at the dog's face to make it stop. But the dog didn't stop at all—it sprang forward like all it wanted in the world was to tear Jerry Lee to pieces, and if it first had to eat a stick to get there, then that was just fine. But the moment the dog leapt was also the moment Jerry Lee jabbed the stick forward, and the blade-like end of the branch disappeared into the dog's open mouth. Jerry Lee could feel the jolt all the way up to his shoulders, and he knew he'd poked through something inside the dog's throat.

The dog thudded to the ground and frantically scooted backward from Jerry Lee toward the safety of the house while blood spurted from its mouth onto the sidewalk stones. It turned and clawed its way back onto the stoop, spraying blood across the concrete and even up along the white siding of the house before it disappeared at last through the open doorway. The woman inside the house screamed.

Jerry Lee crossed to the rock wall and hoisted himself up using Mr. Gatlin's crutch. The woman, probably Mrs. Crabtree, was still screaming as he jumped from the wall. He limped as fast as he could manage across the littered hillside. His mama would spank him for tearing his new jeans, but that couldn't be helped. His leg was beginning to feel like fire, and on any other day he would have cried. But there was no time for that now. The Crabtrees might come after him for killing their dog, and if they did, he'd have to lead them far away. He would circle up through the woods above Mulberry Avenue, then sneak down past the Esso station and come up the creek from the other end. He couldn't let anyone follow him back to the tunnel. Mr. Gatlin might be skittish in the daylight, and if the Crabtrees came around, Mr. Gatlin might disappear. Then the bargain would be broken.

He wondered if dogs could be haints. Maybe Chester's spirit would track Jerry Lee down, like any dog could, and get back at him in the night.

No. He would bring Mr. Gatlin the perfect crutch, and Mr. Gatlin would protect him from Chester and from everything else, even the Enemy. Jerry Lee had made friends with a haint. He'd never have to be afraid of the dark again.

SURFACE TENSION

Lyle stood under the eaves of his garage and stared glumly up at the rain cascading from the roof of his house. The water twined together for the full two-story drop and smacked hard onto the edge of the crumbling driveway. Lyle wondered how the water held together like that, well-defined and tangible as rope. It probably had something to do with surface tension. He remembered his high school chemistry teacher floating a needle in a glass of water and saying surface tension was what made it possible. But he never really knew what that meant. Scientific demonstrations usually impressed Lyle more as magic tricks than as examples of Natural Law.

Part of the overflow problem was in the sagging roof line, which dipped considerably between the end-peaks of the house and curved the guttering into what now appeared to be a thin, drooling smile. There was nothing much he could do about it. Jacking the mid-beams up would be expensive and, in the short run, wouldn't be worth it. He knew he could find a buyer for the place as-is. The shingles still had ten years left in them, which meant he could say they had at least fifteen; and once the pigeon droppings were hosed off, the aluminum siding could almost pass for new.

The pigeons themselves, of course, would have to go. In just three weeks of roosting they'd all but ruined the carpeting on the back patio, and Lyle was sure their feathers and droppings were starting to clog the downspouts, which made the drainage problem even worse. Margie wanted him to leave them alone—

she liked hearing them coo outside the bedroom window every dawn. They were a gentle kind of alarm clock, she said. Lyle might have agreed if they'd been talking about just one or two birds. But yesterday he'd counted more than two dozen sunning themselves above the back porch. They were taking the place over. This morning at breakfast he'd tried again to get Margie to understand the financial realities involved, but she wouldn't listen. She said that killing the birds wouldn't solve any problems. The woman simply had no head for business.

"Pigeons aren't birds," he finally told her. "They're vermin— rats with wings. They drive the property values down. If you want to live in a goddamn wildlife sanctuary, move the hell to Wyoming."

Margie glared at him for a while, then got up from the table and put her plate in the sink. "Fine," she said, and walked out of the room.

It was settled then: the pigeons were to be disposed of. The only question was how to go about it.

A break in the downpour came just as Betzger's Heating and Plumbing van swung into the driveway. Betzger was a buzzy little cigar-chewer who'd barely made it past ninth grade, and Lyle hated to be around him. He hated that Betzger always smelled of stale sweat and the undersides of toilets. He hated that, whatever they talked about, Betzger seemed vaguely disinterested, as if he were about to say, "So what?" He even hated that such an ill-bred gnome could run his own company, drive around town in a hand-waxed van with his name stenciled neatly on the side. But business was business, and right now Betzger was one of the people Lyle had to deal with.

"What's the word, Ed?" he asked, stepping out into the drizzle as Betzger climbed down from the driver's seat. It wasn't a casual question. Lyle had been on the edge of panic ever since the storm front had moved in late Wednesday night, flash flooding his end of the neighborhood and washing out his garden. He was sorry to lose the garden because it might have been a good selling point, but what bothered him more was the rain itself. If it kept up much longer, he might have to cancel his House Hunters' Luau. The Luau was the best promotional idea he'd had in a decade, just the thing to re-energize his real estate business. He'd been in a slump the last year or so. Well, three years, if he were being honest. And he didn't know why. Sure, the housing market had slowed, but that shouldn't be anything to deter to a top-rank salesman like himself. He had the tools, he knew that well enough. For example, he'd always been a great joke teller—a regular raconteur, in fact—and buyers always trust a man who can make them laugh. Still, people didn't seem to take to him the way he imagined they used to. But this Luau thing would fix all that, he was certain of it. They might even write him up in the local paper.

If the rain didn't ruin everything.

He'd spent Thursday morning checking with the local radio stations to find out the chance of thunderstorms for the weekend. They all said the same thing: according to the wire service, the severe weather would be gone by Friday morning. The weekend would be sunny and mild.

But now it was Friday afternoon, the sky had been rumbling and cracking all day, and Lyle was stuck with a deal to take delivery on nine hundred dollars' worth of discount clams.

"Got 'em all right here," said Betzger, smiling and patting the side of his van. "Where you want 'em?"

"I hope you're not serious," said Lyle, forcing a deadpan calm into his voice.

"Just poke your head in the back and take a whiff if you don't believe me."

"But you're a day early." Lyle felt the blood beat harder in his head. "The Luau's not until tomorrow."

"Yeah, I know. The storm's played hell with the fishing schedules. None of the boats have gone out the last couple of days. Bobby said it was either this load or nothing."

"Then why the hell couldn't you wait until tomorrow to deliver it?"

Betzger shrugged. "They might not be so fresh by then. Bobby don't have anything to keep 'em cold."

So Margie had been right. Pay retail, she had told him. If you've got to buy the stupid clams, at least get them from a legitimate outfit, and not from some fly-by-nighter like Betzger's brother-in-law. But Lyle had insisted. Clams are clams, he told her. Now he couldn't even refuse the shipment since he'd paid for it all in advance.

At least Margie wasn't there to gloat. He supposed there was some consolation in that.

"And what am I supposed to do with them until tomorrow?" Lyle demanded.

Betzger looked at him as if the answer were obvious, which of course it was. "Well, if I were you," he said, shoving a fat cigar in his teeth, "I'd stick what I could in the refrigerator. The rest I'd pack in ice."

Yes, this was a reasonable solution, Lyle could see that. There was no real problem at all.

"I can rent you the ice chests," Betzger went on. "But you'll have to supply your own ice. I threw some in the back myself so the van wouldn't get too stunk up, but that's about gone by now."

"Fine," said Lyle, smiling again. He felt good: he was coping now—the pounding in his head had nearly stopped. The sky was clearing, his advertising posters for the party were posted all over town, and the clams were at his door. Margie would see that she'd been wrong.

It still amazed him that she'd been so angry about this whole affair. Apparently, she didn't understand that to make money, first you had to spend a little. And it wasn't like he was renting some fancy ballroom somewhere. He was staging the Luau right here in his own backyard with minimal overhead. A public relations gold mine, that's what he'd conjured up, there was no doubt about it. Suddenly everyone would know who he was. Wealthy, tanned executives and business owners and other one-percenters would slap him on the back, extend invitations, offer him drinks. One of the boys: he'd be one of the boys.

Margie couldn't see it. When he'd broached the subject, she'd stared at him like he was an imbecile.

"We haven't got money to throw away on a party," she said flatly. Then she picked up the *TV Guide* and began to thumb through the listings, as if the matter were already dismissed from her mind.

"Don't think of it like a party," he told her. "It's a business expense. The whole thing's tax deductible."

Margie closed the magazine and placed it carefully on the edge of the kitchen table. "That doesn't change the facts," she said, measuring her words as if she were speaking to a child. Then she slowly clasped her hands and leaned forward in her chair. "We can't afford to do this right now," she said. Lyle hated it when she spoke so methodically. Somehow it made whatever she said seem indisputable. This time, though, he knew she was wrong.

"We can't afford not to," he said. "It's the best way in the world to generate new business."

"You don't know that," she said, the counterfeit of patience still shaping her voice. "All you're talking about is pure blind risk."

Pure blind risk. That was rich. Of course it was pure blind risk. His whole career was pure blind risk. That's what selling was. Why the hell didn't she know that by now? Still, he couldn't blame her for worrying about the money. The local market was tight right now; he hadn't sold a house in over six months. But the Luau would change all that. It would buy him a million dollars' worth of visibility. What did Margie think— that people picked their realtors from the yellow pages? Well, then she had a hell of a lot to learn. The names people trust are the names they've seen and heard most often. The basic groundwork was already laid. He had the billboard on Route 30 just outside of town, the regular ad in the Sunday paper, and free calendars to the church groups every Christmas. He wasn't unknown, not at all. But this clambake deal would make it all finally gel. He'd be back on his feet in no time, and the sky would be the limit. He might even hire somebody to build him a website. Then Margie would put her head on his shoulder and say he'd done the right thing after all.

Well, no. He could never imagine her saying or doing anything of the kind. That wasn't her style, not anymore. But other things were possible. First of all, she'd probably demand that he replace her Volkswagen, which he'd sold to cover the cost of the clams and the beer. That would at least be a start; at least she'd be speaking to him again. Then there might be room to negotiate. That's all he needed. He was a businessman, after all, and marriage was a deal like any other. It was simply a matter of figuring the right trade-offs. This for that, that for this. The secret was in knowing how to give the small things up.

After he'd filled the refrigerator with clams and transferred the remainder into coolers of cold water in the backyard, Lyle was feeling expansive enough to offer Betzger a beer, and the two of them sat down together on the rear bumper of the van. The sun by now had burned away the residual haze of the storm, and the damp air had grown muggy in the heat. The yard would have a full day to dry out, but Lyle doubted whether that would be enough.

Betzger took a long gulp of beer and tapped his foot in the broad puddle at their feet. "I notice you got a drainage problem here." He nodded toward the end of the drive. "You ought to have me dig a runoff line around this low side." He topped his bottle toward the house. "Otherwise, it'll start eating into your foundations."

"There's no place for it to run off to," Lyle told him. "We're the low point of this whole side of town. Everybody else's runoff collects right here."

"That so?" Betzger looked from the house to the street. He pointed to the sewer opening on the far curb. "What about tapping into the main line over there?"

Lyle took a sip of his beer and shook his head. "Half the water in the front yard came out of that sewer. It backs up every time we get a hard rain."

"Well, you ought to do something about it," Betzger said, apparently disturbed by the thought that there was a drainage problem too difficult for him to solve. "Water don't just stand, you know. It seeps."

Lyle knew all about seepage. In the five years they'd lived in the house, he'd never known the basement to be fully dry. There was probably at least an inch of water on the floor right now, maybe more, though he'd made the conscious decision not to check. He didn't have much use for basements anyway.

"The backyard seems in good shape, though," Betzger added, frowning just enough to let Lyle know that what he was offering was not a compliment but a professional appraisal.

"Yeah," said Lyle. "The drainage is a little better there because it's on a rise. The water seems to pool along the back property line, so most of the yard stays pretty firm."

"Where's everybody gonna sit?"

"I rented picnic tables. Hansen's is bringing them out tomorrow."

"Hansen's?" Betzger shook his head. "I could have got you a better deal. Next time let me know. I handle all that kind of stuff for the Kiwanis Club, you know. Whatever you need, I can usually come up with it. You got the boiler and the steam tables already, I guess."

"Yeah."

"Chairs, paper plates, napkins, all that kind of stuff?"

"It's in the garage."

"How many kegs?"

"Six. We might not need that many, but we can take back what we don't tap."

Betzger sighed and took another swallow of beer. "Looks like you've got your bases covered."

More than anything in the world, Lyle wanted to believe that he had his bases covered. But something was wrong. Sellers were known by their product, he knew that. If his own home looked like a dump, who would trust him to tell a good house from a bad one?

The pond in the front yard was really no problem. All he had to do was draw attention to it himself, explain that it was some kind of freak accident. He could say one of the main sewer lines was closed for repairs and too much runoff had been rerouted his way. That would cover it. Instead of thinking he was a fool for buying a house with a drainage problem, they'd all sympathize with him, and probably offer stories about when the same thing had happened to them. They'd all have a good laugh about it.

The sag of the roof line was imperceptible on sunny days when there was no overflow in the guttering to make it obvious; and the flooded basement was a secret easily kept. But if the house were covered with pigeons, ceaselessly pacing the gutters, bobbing their heads and cooing in chorus, no one would believe he was a responsible homeowner. They'd think he was the kind of man who'd let things slide, a man not to be trusted with real estate needs. Clearly, these pigeons could be his downfall.

"Know anything about pigeons?" he asked.

Betzger smiled. "They're all dark meat. Not as good as dove, though. Why?"

Lyle pointed to the roof. The pigeons had already emerged from the shelter of the eaves and were congregating around the old TV antenna. "I've got some to get rid of," he said.

"Lay out a little poison," Betzger suggested.

"Too unpredictable," said Lyle. He knew he couldn't count on these birds eating whatever bait he might set out, at least not in time for them all to drop dead before tomorrow afternoon, and he sure as hell didn't want any stricken pigeons plummeting onto the patio in the middle of the Luau. "I need something quicker, something I can count on."

"Hell, plug 'em."

"Too noisy." Lyle certainly couldn't afford to make such a threatening spectacle of himself. A man who stands on his lawn taking shots at his house is not a man people will do business with. One of the neighbors might even call the police.

Betzger leaned back against the rear door of the van. "Well, when I was a kid, me and a pal used to kill a lot of seagulls down at Rehoboth Beach. You know how they'll swoop down and kind of hover in the air, waiting for tourists to throw some bread or popcorn up in the air? We used to throw Alka-Seltzers. Birds can't belch like people, you know. All that fizz just makes them blow right up." He finished off his beer and set the bottle on the edge of the driveway. "I don't guess that'd work with pigeons, though. They can't hover and they won't catch what you throw at them." He leaned back against the door of the van. "You might could toss a few Alka-Seltzers up there anyway, just for fun. Who knows? They might go for it."

Lyle tossed his own bottle into the grass. "And the next time it rained I'd have foam all over my house."

"Well," said Betzger, squinting up toward the roof, "I could trap 'em easy enough, if you could give me a few weeks. Apart from that, there's not too many options. Bow and arrow, maybe."

As soon as the suggestion left Betzger's lips, Lyle knew it was the answer he'd been looking for. Two dozen fat, filthy pigeons skewered before sundown. He'd always been a good archer with those suction-tipped play sets he'd had when he was a kid. He'd even bought himself a hunting bow for Christmas a few years back, though he'd never gotten around to buying any arrows. The bow was still in the hall closet, waiting.

Lyle stood up and stretched. Bit by bit, the pieces of his life were falling into place. Betzger pulled a fresh cigar from his shirt pocket and bit off the tip.

"Guess I better get back to work," he said, pushing himself up from the bumper. "Let me know if you need anything else."

"I still need a load of ice. If you've got the time."

Betzger studied his watch for a moment and then nodded. "I guess I can handle that," he said. "Shouldn't take more than half an hour."

"Great," said Lyle. "Let's go."

"No need for you to come," said Betzger, pulling open the driver's side door. "It's an easy job. I can do it just as quick by myself."

"I don't mind, really," Lyle insisted. "I need to pick up a couple of things in town."

Betzger lit his cigar and turned toward the empty parking space in the garage. "Something wrong with your car?"

Was there? Lyle tried to think. "It's gone," he said. "My wife took it." He remembered the fantail of water that sprang up from the street as Margie accelerated out of the driveway. He'd never seen her that reckless before. She probably didn't realize how rocky the ride would be if she let the brake pads get wet. He might have to mention it when she got home.

"What about the Beetle?"

"We sold it."

Betzger looked surprised. "I wish I'd known," he said. "I'd have made you an offer on that myself. Those original Bugs are getting to be real collectors' items."

"Yeah, well, we sold it," Lyle said again.

Betzger shrugged. "Come on along then. But I'll have to charge you mileage."

"Fair enough," said Lyle, as he climbed into the passenger side. He truly didn't mind paying for the ride. After all, that's how a free market system worked: supply and demand. Right now Betzger had a seller's market, and he was entitled to get whatever he could out of it. Besides, Lyle always preferred to pay for what he got. Favors made him feel uncomfortable. There were always hidden costs.

In a moment Betzger had them out on the bypass circling up to the north side of town. "Let's get some air in here," he said, cranking down his window. "Try to flush out some of that ocean stink." Lyle lowered his window and let the roar of the wind fill his head. This was nice. He could hardly hear himself think.

"So," Betzger called above the racket, "how long you figure before we get out of this slump?"

Lyle wondered if he'd missed part of a conversation somewhere, something about baseball teams, maybe. "What slump?" he asked.

"Houses," Betzger mouthed around his cigar. "Nobody's buying any houses."

"What do you know about it?" asked Lyle, a little defensively.

"Oh, I stay pretty much in touch with the market. When people buy a house, they'll usually end up having a little plumbing done—either getting new stuff put in or just fixing up whatever the last owners didn't take care of. Same with central air systems."

"So I take it you've had a drop in business lately," said Lyle, trying to keep the conversation away from his own difficulties.

Betzger nodded. "That's why I been hauling seafood for my dipshit brother-in-law. He pays me fifteen percent of the deliveries. Not a bad deal. At least it's something to fall back on."

Lyle turned his face to the wind and watched the shoulder of the road blur past. Something to fall back on. That was a tactic for losers, for people who planned to fail. Falling back meant not moving forward, a life of nickels and dimes. He was glad he had nothing to fall back on. It left him no humiliating choices.

When they got downtown, Lyle had Betzger drop him off at Singleton's Sporting Goods and go on alone to pick up the ice.

"Fifteen minutes!" Betzger called after him, but Lyle was already too preoccupied to answer. He pushed his way through the glass doors and stood breathing in the cool fluorescent air. He loved this. There was magic in retail merchandise, in the buying and selling of brand-name markups, in people making profits and customers feeling satisfied. The clean, oiled smell of it was all around him here, drawing him up and down the aisles, luring him from one display to the next, tempting him with the scores of happy products he wanted but did not need—the gleam of new metal; the polish of leather; the gloss of plastic, vinyl, glass, nylon, rubber; iridescent colors; boxes stacked high. The whole scene shone with a money-back promise of sweaty, mindless play.

"Can I help you with something?" The salesman was a beefy, woodsy-looking fellow with lots of blond hair and an unforced smile. Lyle felt uncomfortable at once.

"I need some archery supplies," he said. "I've already got a bow." He added this so the salesman wouldn't take him for an easy mark.

"Target or game?"

Lyle looked down at his feet and thought hard. "Game," he said finally. "I need arrows and a bowstring."

"How many strands?"

Lyle looked at him blankly.

"We've got ten-, twelve-, fourteen-, and sixteen-strand strings."

"What's the difference?"

"Well, if your bow's got less than a forty-five-pound draw, you can get away with ten or twelve strands. A fourteen-strand string goes with a fifty-five-pound draw. More than fifty-five pounds and you'll need at least a sixteen-strand."

"I'll take the sixteen-strand," Lyle told him, though he had no idea if that was right.

"What length?"

"It stands about this high unstrung," he said, holding his hand at shoulder height.

"That doesn't really pin it down," said the salesman, his smile beginning to broaden. Lyle pictured him with a ski pole through his throat.

"Just give me the longest you've got," he said.

"That'd be sixty inches." The salesman reached into the glass case and selected a small package of thick, black string. He set it on the countertop for Lyle's approval.

"Fine," he said. "And I'll need about fifty arrows."

"Aluminum, steel, fiberglass, or wood?"

"Which is best?"

"Well, the metal tends to hold a truer line, I think. Wood and fiberglass tend to warp when the weather changes."

"I'll take the steel, then."

The salesman opened a thick book and scanned a long row of figures. "Steels are twenty-five dollars a dozen. That's just the raw shafts. Fletching and nocking are extra. And the heads, of course."

"I see."

"Right now we're a little overstocked on helical fletching, so I could give you a good deal there."

"What about the points?"

"Frankly, if you take the helical fletching you can get away with a cheaper head. The torque of the arrow gives you maximum penetration with a simple target point. If you go for the four-sided blade heads, the point itself will keep the arrow on true flight, so you don't really need as much rotation. But it depends on what you're going after. If it's a bear, you want as nasty a head as you can find. If it's a rabbit, you can get by with something a lot simpler, maybe even a blunt point for stunning."

"I want the big heads," Lyle told him. "The ones that look like razor blades."

"I can let you have those for two dollars apiece." He made a few notations on his receipt pad. "How about some camouflage gear?"

"No, I don't think so. I'll just use my old marine fatigues." He had no marine fatigues.

"What about scent? We've got cover-up and lure."

"What do you recommend?"

"Pine oil's a pretty popular cover-up. Some people use skunk oil, but I think a deer or whatever gets suspicious. Skunks don't spray unless there's trouble around, and animals know that. But personally, I'd go with small-animal urine. It's cheap and it's natural." He took a small bottle down from a shelf behind the counter and offered it to Lyle.

"I don't want animal urine," he said. He was sure of this.

The salesman returned it to its place on the shelf and took down a smaller plastic squeeze bottle. "How about standard rut lure, then, if deer's what you're after. Lay a track of this stuff through the woods and bucks will follow you for days. All you've got to do is wait for them to catch up and then show them what Cupid's arrow can really do."

Lyle began to feel sick. "I'm not after deer," he said. "I just want to sell some houses."

The ride back was pleasant. Loading thirty-five bags of crushed ice into the van had apparently worn Betzger down enough to dull his interest in conversation, so Lyle had nothing to do but smile happily ahead, the sack of arrows clutched to his chest. When they pulled to a stop in the driveway, Lyle climbed down from the van and headed immediately for the house, leaving Betzger to unload the ice by himself. Lyle didn't feel guilty. He knew Betzger would charge him plenty for the extra work, and right now time meant more to him than money. The sun was already starting its descent. In another two hours the glare would be directly in his eyes as he sighted on the birds. He could shoot only from the front yard, after all, since the weed lot bordering his back yard was the only place he could drop the arrows safely. He knew he wouldn't get every pigeon this afternoon, but at least he'd have a good head start on tomorrow.

The arrows, it turned out, were easy to assemble, and it wasn't until he'd finished the last one and set it on the pile that he realized fifty arrows was more than he needed. Any misfires could be easily retrieved and shot again. Still, this way would be more convenient, so he didn't feel bad. And luck was with him on the bowstring. He'd planned to tie knots in it to shorten it for his bow, but it turned out he'd bought the right length after all. He bent the bow around the back of his leg like a veteran archer and looped the loose end of the string over the notches. Everything was ready. He gathered the bundle of arrows under his arm and slung the bow across his chest as he'd seen done in the movies. Then he slipped quietly out the back door, thinking to circle around and catch his prey off guard. Betzger had emptied the ice bags into the clam coolers, he noted, and as he rounded the corner of the house he realized the van was gone. He felt oddly alone, as if he'd just been left in the wilderness for a two-week survival course. He stopped for a moment to listen: the neighborhood was quiet except for a faint whir of a distant lawn mower and the trilling coo of the pigeons.

He eased out toward the middle of his front lawn and looked up at the gallery of birds ranged along the roof line. They were all watching him. For the first time he noticed their feathers. Each bird was distinctively glossed with iridescent swirls of color—not like most birds, which seemed merely to be interchangeable versions of one another. Some of these pigeons were beautifully marked. Margie had mentioned that once, he now recalled. She'd even given some of them names. Albert. Red. Scruffy. Slick. Mary Lou. Lyle didn't want to remember which was which.

It had been a long time since he'd used a bow, and it occurred to him that he ought to aim a little high for the first few shots, just until he got his accuracy back. No sense ripping up his shingles. But beyond that single precaution, he realized he had no real strategy of attack. With geese, he knew, it was smart to shoot the birds at the end of the flying formation first so the others wouldn't panic and spread. He doubted whether the same principle applied here, but something about his sense of order told him to start from the left and work his way across, the way he would in a shooting gallery.

Lyle positioned himself so his sight line ran parallel to the slant of the roof, and drew back the bow for his first shot. He held the pose for a moment, focusing on a blue-and-white bird that had paused by the chimney to watch him. He let the arrow fly and watched it soar quickly out of sight. The pigeon seemed undisturbed. Good power, Lyle told himself, not worried that the first shot had failed to come within a yard of the target. He was just finding the range, after all.

The second arrow came no closer than the first, though this time the pigeon hopped and fluttered a bit, as if it now suspected something was up. Lyle pulled the bow back as far as he could and sent the third arrow whizzing toward the roof line. The shot was wide to the right, but another bird blundered up over the crest just at that moment, and the arrow caught him right below the beak, completely removing his head. He flopped forward and tumbled down the incline, snagging briefly on the guttering before a final spasm propelled him over the edge and onto the boxwood in the yard below. Lyle stepped up and looked at the headless bird lying cushioned by the springy branches. It was Slick, his colors still shimmering on his back like the rings of an oil spill.

Lyle felt vaguely disturbed, as if he were a trespasser in his own front yard. The accidental nature of the kill made it all the more grotesque, and now every thought in his head seemed suddenly guilty and unnatural. He needed Margie here to tell him what was wrong.

The other pigeons seemed largely unconcerned. A few rose and flapped to the top of the chimney or circled away to the rear of the house, but most stayed right where they were.

Lyle eased out farther in the yard to get a better angle against the increasing glare and set another arrow to the bowstring. Again he pulled the bow back as far as he could, bringing the silvery blades of the head almost to his fingers. He leveled his aim on a stark white bird perched on the gutter by the downspout, a bird Margie had not yet named. For a long moment Lyle held the pigeon in his sights, staring up the shaft to the round, plump breast. A tightness crept through his arms and across his chest, and suddenly he'd waited too long, the strain was too great, the bow began to quiver. Still, he held the arrow back, his fingers tight against the string, so tight they hurt, so tight a numbness took them over, freezing them in place, as if they weren't a part of him at all. He took a sharp breath and strained again against the bow, and now his fingers unlocked, the bowstring snapped away, and the arrow flew up hard against the house, the head slicing through the aluminum siding.

The pigeons rose with a start and swept away to the stand of trees beyond his neighbor's house, disappearing quietly into the topmost branches.

Lyle stared up at the ruined siding, unable to believe what he'd done. But there it was, the feathered shaft protruding from his outer bedroom wall. How could he explain a thing like that? What would Margie say?

He dropped the bow and walked to the edge of the porch where he could better gauge the damage. The arrow was in deep, and he guessed the razored head would be sticking through the plaster just above the picture Margie had hung on that wall—the small blurry photo of the two of them on the beach at Dauphin Island. It was the only picture they had from their honeymoon, taken by a man with a Polaroid who'd charged them two dollars. Their own camera had been lost when the sailboat Lyle had rented capsized in choppy water.

He knew she had always blamed him for that, and remembering it now, he supposed he hadn't used his best judgment. He'd wanted to impress her, but he'd never sailed before and, without realizing what he was doing, he steered the boat broadside to the wind. Lyle managed to scramble up over the side of the boat as it rolled, but Margie had gone into the water with the mast on top of her and for a moment she was held under, caught beneath the sail. But only for a moment—Lyle pulled her out, then righted the boat and drew her back on board. "We're all right," he told her, but she was hysterical and slapped his hands away. She said he had no business taking them out where a thing like this could happen. He was surprised she could be so furious, and he kept silent as he maneuvered the craft toward shore, worried the whole way back that he might tip them over again. They were both relieved when the hull finally scudded into the soft updrift of the beach, but for a long time neither of them moved from the boat, or even spoke. "It was just an accident," he said at last. "That's no excuse," she told him. Why wasn't it? he wondered, though he felt afraid to ask.

Now she would see this arrow as one more piece of evidence against him. It wasn't fair. She had no right to blame him for things he'd never meant to do. But she would blame him, and now he felt more guilty than if he'd shot the house on purpose. His face felt chilled, as if he'd run too far, too fast, and turned his own sweat cold. He could feel the blood beating in his head.

He had almost mustered the courage to go inside when Margie wheeled their Plymouth through the pool of water at the foot of the driveway and pulled up in front of the garage. There was no use pretending he hadn't seen her—she'd only get suspicious—so he sat casually on the edge of the stoop and waited for her to join him.

"Hello," she said. Her face was still pretty, even without a smile.

"Hi." He liked her dress. It was blue with little flecks in it, like a robin's egg.

"I came back to get some of my things." He liked her gold earrings, too, but they made her look too formal for this time of day. Her hair—was there something different about her hair? He couldn't tell.

"Sure," he said. "Fine."

She sighed and walked past him into the house.

Lyle couldn't believe his luck. Slick was lying right there, headless, in the branches of the boxwood and she hadn't even noticed. He didn't think she'd seen the bow and arrows, either. If he could just get everything out of sight, she might never know what he'd been up to. Of course, she was bound to see the arrow in the bedroom wall, but when she asked him about it, he could act surprised. "Must have been vandals," he'd tell her. Kids today were just that crazy—she'd have to believe him. Sure, everything would work out fine.

He shoved the bird deep inside the bush and hurried out into the yard to gather the equipment. The sewer was a likely place, especially for the arrows; he wasn't sure whether the fiberglass bow would float or not, but he figured he could stuff it far enough down the opening that it wouldn't matter.

As he waded along the curb, feeling for the storm drain with his feet, he kept an eye on their bedroom windows. There was no sign of Margie. He smiled. She had probably decided to start fixing dinner. In a little while she'd open the door and call him inside. He'd say something nice to her then, maybe ask about her hair. By then he'd have everything back under control. She'd never suspect a thing.

MULE COLLECTOR

The new mule pushed his way in among the others and pressed his muzzle tentatively against the sparkling walls of Glen L. Hanshaw's glassed-in patio. Glen L. stood for a moment in the kitchen doorway, iced tea in hand, admiring the scene around him. All six of his mules were out there, spaced irregularly around the patio's three exposed sides, running their lips and tongues along the sticky surface, sometimes clacking their big teeth against the shatter-resistant glass. Even through the smeared slobber that partly clouded his view, he could see the inner workings of the mouths, the jaws moving in a chorus of silent conversation, telling him things that only mules could know.

He moved methodically across the flagstone floor and eased himself into the webbing of his lounge chair, careful not to spill too much of his tea. He'd overextended himself today, first on the golf course and then with the mules, and now even the mild strain of steadying his full glass brought tremors from some fault line in his legs or back or brain. He set the tea on the floor beside him and closed his eyes to rest.

The tournament had taken more out of him than he'd expected. He'd ridden in a cart, of course, but, even so, a full eighteen holes was more than he was used to these days. He'd fallen into the habit of playing only abbreviated rounds—starting at the fourth hole, which ran parallel to his mule field, and finishing on the seventh green just across the fairway from his house. Maybe a two-day tournament was more than he could handle. Already he felt the muscles along the backs of his legs and arms stiffening like old leather, and the thought of having to play another full round tomorrow gave him a sudden chill.

Or was that the air-conditioning? The blistering heat on the course today had baked him like a clay pot, so as soon as he'd made it back to the house, even before tending to the mules, he'd cranked the thermostat into the blue arctic range. Now goosebumps rose from his raw patches of sunburn. That was all right, though. He enjoyed being uncomfortably cold on the hottest day of the year. That's what being rich was all about.

For their part, the mules seemed perfectly content, the half dozen of them ranged in the long shade of the house, pressing their gums against the cool, sweet glass. They knew how to tolerate the heat, how to pace themselves against the mercury, moving only when they had a better place to go. Glen L. hadn't understood that as a boy. He remembered walking the plow behind his father's big pair of drays, breaking sod for a late-summer crop. On hot days the mules worked more slowly, keeping him longer in the fields, and he had hated them for that. But now he understood their stubbornness: a bad sun called for a slower pace, plain and simple. Why hadn't he known that back then?

"Hey, Dad! Are you home?" The voice startled him, and Glen L. suddenly remembered that he wasn't alone in the house this weekend. One of his sons had come to visit, and they were partners in the member-guest. But what the hell was his name?

"I'm out here," Glen L. called. "On the patio."

"I got us a couple of steaks, and all the fixings," the boy announced from the kitchen. Glen L. heard the papery rattle of grocery sacks being dumped on the counter.

Harold, that was it: the boy's name was Harold. Bill was the one who was dead.

"I thought you'd be going to the tournament barbecue," Glen L. called. "It's already paid for."

"I'm not much on pork ribs," Harold said. He stepped out onto the patio. "I thought maybe we'd get out the grill. . ."

Glen L. looked up at his son: not a boy anymore, but a fat, bald fifty-year-old with broken blood vessels mapping his cheeks and nose, his mouth now hanging open like a clubbed fish. But Harold wasn't a fish. He was something more lamentable, more obsolete. A 1966 Chevy Corvair barreling flat-out for the scrap heap. But how could that be? How could a son of his be such an old man already? And where did that leave Glen L.?

"Jesus Christ," Harold muttered. "What the hell's going on out here?"

"I'm watching my mules."

"But, I mean—" he gestured toward the smeared walls, "what the hell are they doing?"

"They're licking the glass," Glen L. told him. He pointed to the small plastic bucket and broad-bristled paint brush stationed by the patio door. "I coat the walls with wet sugar every afternoon. It's their special treat."

Harold sat down heavily in the Barcalounger. "But it's grotesque." He scanned the row of mules uneasily, his blue eyes bright and watery like his mother's.

"The mules seem to like it," Glen L. said, reaching down for his tea. "Especially the new one. I think the group activity helps him fit in."

"New one?" Harold scowled through a quick count, then shook his head. "Christ, Dad, you can't keep doing this."

Glen L. smiled. "I found an old sugar mule over in Able County. Got a great deal. Sugar mules are pretty rare around here. The farmer didn't even know what he had—thought it was a *cotton* mule. Can you imagine that?"

Harold sighed and reached over to steady the cut-crystal glass in Glen L.'s hand. "Here, let me help you," he said, lifting it away, and Glen L. realized he'd sloshed some tea across the front of his shirt. He wiped at it clumsily with his fingers, pressing the cold spill against his stomach. When he looked up, Harold was standing by him with a roll of paper towels.

"Now I'm in the market for a couple of good pack mules," he said, dabbing a wad of towels along the stain. "But this is the wrong part of the country, so I might have to wait a while."

Harold cleared his throat and stared at the mule directly in front of him, a male Missouri with crooked, blackened teeth. "Six mules is a pretty big responsibility."

Glen L. snorted. "Six? Six is nothing. You know what my inventory is down at the car lot? I can show you sixty brand new Cadillacs any goddam day of the year."

"I know, Dad. But running the dealership isn't the same thing as filling up your yard with mules. I don't think you can equate the two."

Glen L. felt a flare of anger. What the hell way was that for a son to talk to his father? *I don't think you can equate the two.*

Like some schoolteacher talking to a backward kid. If Glen L. had ever said anything like that to his own father, he'd have felt a leather strap across his backside. "I can equate anything I want," he said, though he knew that was a lie.

He could never equate Harold and Bill, for example. Bill had been a born salesman, like his father, and could have done anything—run his own company, maybe, or had his own TV show, or even gone into politics. But Harold had become—what was it again?—some kind of accountant. An actuarial accountant, that was it, working in a sunless office up at the state capitol. Gray rooms and long numbers and cold marble floors. True, Glen L. had never actually seen the place; but he'd been there in his mind, and it felt just like a morgue.

Harold stepped over to the glass wall and drummed his fingers lightly above the Missouri mule's head, but the animal didn't seem to notice.

"Don't get them started," Glen L. warned.

Harold stopped tapping the glass. "What do you mean?"

"I mean they're quiet now, but if you spook one he'll start to bray. And if one starts, the others are liable to join in. That'll make one hell of a racket." He smiled at the thought. The truth was, he loved it when his mules got rowdy. Of course, from time to time a few upstarts from the Country Club complained about the noise, but that didn't worry him. It was his club, after all. He'd helped found it back in '48, and had written most of the bylaws himself. For the last twenty years, he'd even been club president. Let the new members grouse all they wanted—he knew the board would never dare take him on.

"Sorta like a zoo, isn't it," Glen L. said. "Except we're the ones inside. That makes it better, I think."

"Sure," said Harold, but from the way he chewed his lower lip Glen L. could see he wasn't sure at all. Lip-chewing was a giveaway Harold had inherited from his mother—a skittish woman, really, overly polite, who almost never spoke her mind. For thirty-eight years she'd kept her conversations with Glen L. on a sort of cruise control set below the speed limit, and he had learned to look for meanings in her face, rather than her words. "How are you feeling?" he would ask, and she'd always say, "Fine," even in the end, when her body made it clear she was dying.

Glen L. reached again for his glass of tea, and with a concentrated effort lifted it smoothly to the armrest of his chair.

"Remember the time I took you boys to the Washington Zoo?" he asked. "Nineteen-fifty-six. We saw the real Smokey the Bear. I bet you forgot about that."

Harold smiled. "No, I remember," he said easing himself back into the Barcalounger. "We fed him a bag of peanuts."

"That's right. You boys fed peanuts to Smokey the Bear. That's something to be proud of. It's like being part of American history."

"Well, I guess. . ."

"Then we went to Mount Vernon. Drove out there in the snow. Had just about the whole damn place to ourselves."

"And froze our butts off," Harold said.

Glen L. frowned and waved the notion away as if it were a puff of smoke. "That part doesn't matter." He leaned over sideways and took a careful sip of tea. "You know, this instant mix is pretty good stuff. It's got the sugar and the lemon already in it. You don't have to do a thing but add water."

"Uh, yeah, I think I've had it before."

"The thing I hate about regular iced tea is you can't ever get the sweetness right. No matter how hard you stir, the sugar won't ever dissolve, it just swirls around a while and then sinks to the bottom." He lifted the glass briefly between them. "But this stuff is great," he said, and for a long moment they both stared at the sweating half-glass of tea, almost as if they expected it to do something.

"Maybe I'll have some later," Harold said, finally.

Glen L. suddenly remembered why he'd brought up Mount Vernon. "George Washington was the first commercial mule breeder in America," he announced. "I bet you didn't know that."

Harold looked at him suspiciously. "I didn't think you could breed mules," he said. "I thought mules were all sterile."

Glen L. shook his head. "Christ, Harold, did you just fall off the turnip truck? What I mean is he imported jackasses to crossbreed with his mares." He sighed and wiped the back of his wrist across his lips. "Anyway, only the males are guaranteed sterile. Your grandfather had a female hinny once that turned out to be fertile." He paused. "But I guess you don't even know what a hinny is."

Harold shrugged. "Some kind of mule, I guess."

A slow smile smoothed the wrinkles from Glen L.'s lips. "It's exactly like a mule. In fact, you probably couldn't tell the difference in a million years. But," he said, widening his eyes to emphasize the mystery, "it's not really a mule at all. Not in the least." He settled his head back against the chair webbing, satisfied that he'd just given Harold the clue he needed to make his way properly through life.

Harold didn't appear to notice. "You seem to know a lot about mules," he said.

"More than I ever knew about cars." Harold wouldn't believe him, of course, but it was true. After forty years of owning the local Cadillac franchise, he still couldn't explain the difference between one car and another. Oh, he could sell them, all right—but that didn't mean much. He supposed that was the secret most salesmen lived with—that the talent to sell was a thing in itself and could live, even thrive, with no real connection to the product. In Glen L.'s case, he had memorized the options lists and the names of all the technical features that complicated each new model's engine, but rarely had he comprehended even the simplest mechanical workings behind the words. In his own driving, the most basic forms of car maintenance had remained alien to him—things other people might consider routine, like changing an oil filter, or tightening a fan belt, or replacing a wiper blade. In fact, it had always been a point of pride with him that whenever the slightest thing went wrong with whatever car he was driving, he'd just turn it over to his mechanics and pick another demo from his endless stock of cars. And he never used the self-serve gas pumps.

But mules were something he had studied all his life—or at least it seemed that way to him now.

"Pretty soon you won't see any mules at all except in zoos," Glen L. said, pushing himself up from his chair. "There's just no call for them anymore. It's all tractors now."

Harold rose quickly and steadied Glen L. by the elbow, then caught the glass of tea as it slid from the aluminum armrest. Glen L. looked at the rescued drink in Harold's hand, then up at his son's sad eyes, and felt things going wrong inside. The stepstones in his mind seemed suddenly too far apart, and he couldn't make the leaps. "Too fast," he said, meaning he had stood up quicker than he should and had been swamped in a blood-rush of dizziness. This had happened to him frequently, he knew that much. Brief spells of confusion, always worse when he was tired. Hardening of the arteries, that's what they used to call it when a mind slowed down enough to lose its way.

These days they probably had a dozen labels for troubles in the brain—names as specific as Oldsmobile and Chrysler, each with its own set of options. In the end, he imagined, they were all more or less interchangeable. Besides, it hardly mattered what name his problems went by—medical terms were just as meaningless to him as the numbers on an engine.

"That's progress, I guess," said Harold, offering a weak smile, and Glen L. saw that whatever he'd just said to his son must have been misunderstood. He tried to speak again, concentrating hard to keep the words from turning into strangers, from unforming themselves on the tip of his tongue and stalling him in silence. But the dizziness came again like a cool, damp cloth behind the eyes, wiping his thoughts clean. He cleared his throat and tried again, certain he had to say something, even if it made no sense. Awkward pauses made customers uneasy, and that was bad for business.

"What is it you're here for?" he heard himself asking. *What is it you're here for?* Glen L. turned the sound of it over in his mind. Yes, it was a good, sincere question. He knew Harold had come to stay with him for a couple of days, but the reason had momentarily escaped him. Asking about it seemed only logical, a simple step to steady him with a frame of reference. But Harold only blinked and turned his gaze toward the floor. It was his guilty look, and even though Glen L. couldn't immediately sort out the language to say so, he could see that the boy felt stung, as if the question had gone deeper than he'd intended.

"Let's talk about it later," Harold said.

"No such thing," Glen L. snapped. Hadn't this boy learned anything from his old man's four decades in sales? There was no later; later was a sham, a sidestep, a customer's excuse, a pitch gone wrong. It meant no deal, no dice, no chance in hell.

"I just thought it might be better to talk some other time." Harold waved a chubby finger toward the line of mules. "You know—when there aren't so many distractions. What I want to say is kinda serious."

"Everything's serious," Glen L. said. "Rebates, dealer prep, destination charges, factory incentives. Everything." He wasn't sure that was quite what he meant to say, but it was close enough.

Harold raised his head and looked steadily at him. Glen L. tried to meet his gaze, but suddenly shivered, recalling an expression in his own father's eyes, that same look of—what? What was it he saw there? Weariness? Disappointment? Or maybe something else, something Glen L. couldn't remember the word for. Maybe there was no word. But it was a dark look, and it had always made him feel small and troublesome, a boy who somehow didn't measure up. What right did Harold have to wear that look? It wasn't a son's look at all.

"Well, I'm just a little worried, is all," Harold said.

Glen L. nodded. "My mules," he said, and stepped away from his chair to the streaked patio wall. The animals had finished licking away the sugar coating, and stood now staring sleepily ahead into the cool blue tint of the glass. Beyond the mules, Glen L. could see a late foursome trudging up the fourth fairway through the now-broken afternoon heat, and he felt a wave of contentment. He loved living by the Country Club. It gave him a view greener than his own father's farm. So quiet and picturesque—like a postcard of some foreign land.

Emily had been happy enough here, he felt sure of that. Happy as she could have been, anyway. Some people were born to be alcoholics and some people weren't, that was the way Glen L. saw it. Maybe it was genetics or maybe it was some other stroke of fate, but whatever the case, there was nothing anybody could do about it. There was certainly nothing Glen L. could have done about it. Emily had just been one of the unlucky ones. That wasn't Glen L.'s fault.

It wasn't even Bill's fault, though that would have been an easy place to put the blame, with his killing himself like that. Killing himself. That was the one thing Emily never could get past. Of course, Bill hadn't done it on purpose. He'd slipped, that was all. Glen L. was sure of that. All kids played on water towers, and sometimes accidents happened. There was no reason in the world for Bill to have jumped.

And the boys, too, they'd loved living here and having the room to romp as far and wild as they pleased. The yard had been unfenced in those days—no mules to keep in. Though there might have been a dog.

"It's not only the mules, Dad. I'm just not sure you can keep on living by yourself like this. You're not—well, you're not as sharp as you used to be. You need somebody to look after you."

Harold stopped talking then, and in the space that opened between them, Glen L. gradually assembled Harold's meaning.

It crystallized slowly, like a ball of ice, growing clear and hard in his mind. The more he thought, the more he understood; and the more he understood, the colder he got. Harold wanted him put away, that was the gist of it. After all he had done for this boy, Harold wanted him hauled off to the dump like some rusted-out junker. Well, by God, he wouldn't have it. Glen L. had never needed anybody, his family included, and he'd be damned if he'd let a son of his tell him what to do with his life. Maybe Emily would have put up with that kind of disrespect, letting her precious boys say and do whatever the hell they wanted—but not him. No, by God, no son could talk that way and get away with it—that was the one thing he'd learned from his own father. He'd teach this boy who ought to be put away. He'd whip the sonofabitch until he bled. Glen L. could still do that, he still had the right. He'd show this little shit which one of them was boss.

He groped along the top of his trousers for his belt, but couldn't find it. Someone had taken it from him, and he hadn't even noticed. What the hell was happening to him? He began to panic.

"What is it, Dad?" Harold asked, putting his hand lightly on the side of Glen L.'s arm. Glen L. flinched at the touch. Snake. Harold was a goddamn snake. "What's wrong?"

"Need my belt," Glen L. stammered. "Need—" He patted desperately at his stomach and hips, but it was no use. His belt was gone, and his words were failing. He couldn't argue, and he couldn't punish. The rage rose up in him, huge and spiteful, but found nowhere to go. A gulping sob broke from his throat, and he closed his eyes tight, fighting for control.

"It's all right," Harold told him. "You didn't wear a belt today. These pants have an elastic waist, see?" Harold hooked a finger in the top of Glen L.'s pants and tugged. The waistline stretched like a rubber band, then snapped back smartly into place.

As Glen L. stared down at the front of his plaid, elastic pants, he felt the blood surging in his head, and the instant he felt it, he knew his thoughts were scattering again, that some unfathomable tide had swept over him, dragging his mind away from whatever he'd been struggling with. His anger, unmoored from its source, flaked apart like old sheet metal, and he felt suddenly calm again, pleasantly lightheaded, with no particular need to sort through the fragments that remained. He had asked a question about his belt, he remembered, and Harold had answered him; Glen L. had no belt, and it was all right. Why had he worried about his belt, he wondered? It had something to do with Harold—Harold had said something wrong. But what did the belt have to do with it? Harold had teased him about his pants. That was probably it—they really were pretty silly-looking off the golf course. Well, no matter. No harm done. Harold was always putting his foot in his mouth. He never had the gift of gab like his brother Bill. That Bill was a born salesman. Poor Harold couldn't make a pitch if his life depended on it. But they were both good boys.

Funny that he couldn't call to mind how Bill had died. It might have had something to do with cars—an accident of some kind. But maybe not; maybe he was only mixing up parts of the past. Anyway, it would come back to him sooner or later. The important things always drifted back, sometimes even after he'd stopped expecting them.

Looking out across the golf course now, he remembered why Harold had come home to visit. They were partners in the member-guest, just like last year and the year before. Just like every year since the tournament began. They'd actually won it a couple of times, back in their salad days. Harold had once been a pretty fair golfer. Better even than Bill.

"These tournaments are rough on an old man," he said cheerily. "How about you pick us up some steaks, and we'll bring out the grill tonight."

"Sounds pretty good," Harold told him.

"Did you get a chance to check the leaderboard before you left the club?"

"Yeah, I checked it."

"How're we doing?"

"We're doing fine, Dad."

"Within striking distance?"

"Absolutely."

"Well, don't stay out too late tonight. Tomorrow we'll make our move."

The shadows were lengthening now, and Harold switched on the floor lamp by the patio table. A shiver of movement passed among the mules, and as Glen L. turned again to watch them, he saw his own faint outline hovering in the glass. Then his eyes focused on the gently swaying mules, and for a moment he forgot why they were there.

This wasn't the view he'd expected his life to come to. He'd expected to pass his days sitting on the patio with Emily, the two of them watching their grandkids tear across the neatly trimmed lawn. He'd even imagined putting in a pool for days like this. But now he was an old man with brittle bones, and the lawn was a ruin, cut to pieces by the sharp trampling of hooves. There was no pool, there were no grandkids, there was no Bill, there was no Emily. Harold was his only remnant. Glen L. might as well have been a mule himself, for all he'd leave behind him in the world.

Glen L. took his iced tea from Harold's hand and gulped down the last few sugary swallows. His dizziness had passed for now, and he felt clearheaded, more like his old self. But the spells weren't over, he knew that. If anything, they'd come more often now, stealing treasures from his mind like so many pickpockets, each theft so smooth he might not ever know what he had lost.

Was that a good thing, or a bad?

He looked at Harold, who stood in the kitchen doorway now with his fingers laced beneath his belly as if he were holding himself up. "You need to take better care of yourself, Harold," he said. "You look like death on a shingle." Harold smiled, almost like a boy again, and for a moment Glen L. felt younger, too. "Let's kick up our heels," he said, and before Harold could even ask what he meant, Glen L. turned toward the mules and banged the heavy iced tea glass sharply against the patio wall, rattling the panel in its frame. The new sugar mule jerked its head violently to the side, knocking the bad-tempered Missouri in the teeth. The startled Missouri let out a bray and shoved itself sideways against the line of mules to give itself more room to fight. The still-panicked sugar mule drew its head upright and tried to retreat from the wall, but stepped into the fetlock of the dray on its other side. The dray nipped the sugar mule viciously on the shoulder, and now all three mules began to slam back and forth against the line. In a matter of moments nearly all the mules were stumbling sideways in confusion, stepping all over one another, snapping and kicking, braying angrily at the disruption in their lives.

Glen L. leaned forward against the cool plate glass. It was a thrilling spectacle, better than Mount Vernon or the Washington Zoo, better than anything he could ever remember seeing. "It's like a piece of American history," he said happily as his son pulled him back from the glass.

They were all singing now, all six of them, and they'd never been in finer form. Their clamor echoed through the porch, raw-edged and harsh, but still oddly tuneful, a sassy chorus crowding out the air. It was the most complicated sound Glen L. could imagine—far more complicated than the chugging of an engine; more complicated even than the salvaging of lost words.

In some ways it was ugly, like a hopeless pain worming between the ribs.

But that wasn't all of it, not by a long shot. It was a good sound, too—solid and strong, with a wild streak flashing crazily through its heart. If he closed his eyes and listened without thinking, it lodged in his bones like something native, something inborn, something older than his father's oldest mule.

In those ways, it sounded like laughter.

Clint McCown has published four novels and six collections of poems. The only two-time recipient of the American Fiction Prize, he has also received the Midwest Book Award, the Sister Mariella Gable Prize, the Society of Midland Authors Award, the Germaine Breé Book Award, a National Endowment for the Arts grant, an Academy of American Poets Prize, a Barnes & Noble Discover Great New Writers designation, and a Distinction in Literature citation from the Wisconsin Library Association. In journalism, he received an Associated Press Award for Documentary Excellence for his investigations of Organized Crime and political corruption. He has also worked as a screenwriter for Warner Bros. and as a Creative Consultant for HBO Television. He is a former principal actor with the National Shakespeare Company, and several of his plays have been produced. He has received three Notable Essay citations in the *Best American Essays* series. His poems, essays, and stories have appeared in over seventy-five national journals and magazines. He has edited a number of literary magazines, including *Indiana Review* and the *Beloit Fiction Journal*, which he founded. He currently teaches in the MFA program at Virginia Commonwealth University and in the Vermont College of Fine Arts low-residency MFA program. In 2021 he was inducted into the Writers Hall of Fame at Wake Forest University.

9 7